THE DUKE'S LADY

Duke Dare, Book 4

Eliana Piers

ARE YOU SIGNED UP FOR DRAGONBLADE'S BLOG?

You'll get the latest news and information on exclusive giveaways, exclusive excerpts, coming releases, sales, free books, cover reveals and more.

Check out our complete list of authors, too!

No spam, no junk. That's a promise!

Sign Up Here

www.dragonbladepublishing.com

Dearest Reader;

Thank you for your support of a small press. At Dragonblade Publishing, we strive to bring you the highest quality Historical Romance from some of the best authors in the business. Without your support, there is no 'us', so we sincerely hope you adore these stories and find some new favorite authors along the way.

Happy Reading!

CEO, Dragonblade Publishing

Additional Dragonblade books by Author Eliana Piers

Duke Dare Series
The Duke's Spinster (Book 1)
The Duke's Goddess (Book 2)
The Duke's Hellion (Book 3)
The Duke's Lady (Book 4)

CHAPTER ONE

1816 England

S HE WAS THE helper. The sidekick. The nurturer. The one off to the side offering a gentle word of encouragement or reproof, depending on what the situation called for. She was good at it too.

Until there was no one close to her to help anymore.

Zenobia ran her fingers over the barrel of the gun in desperate need of shooting practice. The house party was over and she would be home in a few hours, but she couldn't resign herself to sitting in the carriage just yet. It wasn't a long ride home, but it was just long enough that she wanted to delay the confinement for a short while by getting some much needed exercise.

Besides, when was the last time she was unable to hit a bullseye? Never. And that wasn't bragging, that was the God's honest truth. Since she first started shooting, she had an eye for hitting exactly what she wanted. After that, it was a simple matter of deciding what she wanted to aim for. Because, to be perfectly transparent, aiming for the bullseye every time got rather old. It was sometimes much more diverting to aim for a small mark on the target that only she knew she had picked out. Then when she hit, she could celebrate her self-acknowledged victory.

Though it left others wondering at her skill, that wasn't the point. Nobi was never about being the center of attention or receiving accolades. She was good at what she did for the sheer pleasure of getting it right. For herself.

After a while, her sisters had caught onto her tactics, but they were the only ones who knew about it.

And they always knew that she hit what she targeted. It was just her way. If she didn't get it on the first try, then she'd take a second, and possibly a rare third if the target called for it. So now…the fact that she hadn't been able to hit her target was muddling her mind.

As she marched toward the target practice, she couldn't help but recall the slow descent of accuracy in her shooting over the summer. It was as though with each of her three sisters being matched (and therefore leaving her), her ability to accurately aim a gun was also abandoning her.

Dash it all! It was vexing to have her skills so contingent upon the relationship statuses around her.

Especially when she preferred order, consistency, routine, loyalty. Nobi was the one who never missed chocolate in the morning, tea in the afternoon, and sherry in the evening. Come to think of it, her life revolved around drinks a little too much.

When she needed someone to talk to, she always counted on her sisters. But slowly, one by one, they had each found love earlier this year. Coincidentally, they had each found love in a brave attempt to encourage *her* to pursue love. Essentially, the love of her life, in fact. Right. Well…she wasn't sure she would ever be ready for what that entailed because the only love she knew, she couldn't have.

Now her sisters were gone. Practically. Boudicca was on her honeymoon, hopefully coming home soon. Mimi may as well be on her honeymoon, since she only married yesterday. And Joan was engaged; therefore, she was spending all her time with her betrothed.

At least she still had Chris. Though she couldn't find him this morning. She had intended to say goodbye before she left, but she hadn't been able to find him anywhere. They were friends, so she knew she would see him soon. All the same, she had wanted to talk with him about Mimi and Sam's recent nuptials. She was pretty sure they were a perfect match, though at first it hadn't seemed that way. And she wanted to hear Chris's opinion on it again. Even though they had talked about it several times already…now, she wanted his opinion on it post-wedding. How did they look during the ceremony? Was it as beautiful as she thought it was? What did Chris think about it all?

Yes. Chris. About him…she didn't really feel like thinking about him anymore. For the moment. Especially given how many moments they had shared recently. It was nice. Nice. It. Was. Nice.

She told herself again even as a small pain prickled through her chest. They were friends. And they had just been spending extra time together at this house party considering the relationship statuses of her sisters. Everyone was paired up, leaving Chris and Nobi the leftover singles pair.

Again with the relationship statuses. That's all that had been on her and her sisters' minds since the ridiculous duke dare. Snag a duke, they said. With a laugh and a sip of alcohol that was far too strong for the sororal lightweights.

Well, it had all been in good fun. And Nobi was happy—yes, happy, no, elated—that her sisters had all found love. It was nothing short of a miracle. Three sisters with three young, handsome dukes. Miraculous, indeed. So of course she was ecstatic that they found good men.

She could hardly contain her euphoria. In fact, her delirious happiness was driving her to shoot a gun.

March. March. March.

She was nearly there. There she could take aim and blast away whatever *happiness* she was feeling.

Nobi looked up at the targets and noticed one was a bit off kilter. Wanting to practice on a perfect target was essential to rebuilding her confidence, so she ambled over to the target to recenter it. As she walked, her fingers brushed over the unique embellishment on the pistol's handle again.

Just as she reached the target, she overheard some voices behind the large trees bordering the property. Even at the first words they spoke, she knew they were trouble. She held her pistol to her chest. Their voices were harsh, crude. Maleficent. A cackle for a laugh wrenched through the air, but it didn't float anywhere, it stabbed at anything in its path. These men were ruffians, and they were up to no good. But she was alone with little protection. Thank God for her gun, though they probably had one too. What if they saw her and thought she was spying on them? Her stomach churned aggressively inside of her, like a tidal wave she had only read about. And she was a tiny boat sailing across what she thought were smooth waters. But no, the waters were violent. Which only meant one thing…she needed to find out what they were doing here.

Her insides were jostling about, and she instinctively felt as though she might cast up her accounts. Of one thing she was sure, there was no chance in hell she was shooting her pistol while they stood so close. There was no way she wanted to make them aware of her presence.

She was just close enough to hear them, but the trees and bushes were thick, so they couldn't see her. Something about their tone signaled that they were about to divulge important news about the nefarious plans they had at play, so she quieted her breath and calmed her pulse. In the same manner that she would do to take a more challenging shot, and then she listened.

"You're sure he's here?" A gruff voice asked in annoyance.

Nobi stood perfectly still waiting for the reply. She didn't want to breathe, she was so nervous. Afraid that at the tiniest movement, all those butterflies swarming her stomach would unleash and escape, thus drawing attention to her whereabouts.

And worse, they might turn on her gut instead.

"I'm sure, I'm sure. He's here," an equally abrasive baritone responded.

"You better be right. I don't want to waste my time. Again."

The voice answered in an increased pitch and volume, with a slight tremor like a witch might have. "Again? You must be out of your mind. Last time was your fault."

"I didn't say it wasn't."

Oomph! The second voice let out a small cry of pain. Or perhaps wounded dignity. "No need to rough me up before we nab him. You know I bruise easily."

"Don't be a peach. I'll do whatever I want to."

For a second time, the man that she could only envision as lankier than the other let out an Oomph! "Knock it off. If we're going to grab this man, we both need to be ready for him. I hear he's strong."

Nobi's heart plummeted to her toes and rose up again on a wave. Who were they going to take? She needed to listen longer in hopes that they might say his name. There were only a few people left at the house party. Then she remembered that a few had left last night. Perhaps they had missed their target. She could only hope.

"Aye. That's why we're going to knock him out and tie him up, you idiot."

"Don't call me that. You know I'm sensitive."

"Aww shut up. Fine. I didn't mean it, you sensitive ape." One of them must have pushed the other, because a slight shuffling of feet and a grunt could be heard before the man continued, "Now be alert. The word is that they're all leaving the party this morning. We should see him shortly. Then we'll just follow his carriage until he's out of view and grab him."

"Are you sure he hasn't left already?" The first voice was sure a whiny fellow considering his career choice.

"I got eyes, you dolt. I think I would have noticed his carriage."

Something about that sentence struck Nobi in the gut, like it should mean more to her than it did in the moment.

"I'm not a dolt."

"You forgot your gun, didn't you? That's what I thought. You had one job."

"Two. I had two jobs. Ha! At least I can count. And I didn't fail in the other. I brought the rope."

"Well at least you got that right." Harrumph. "We'll be fine. It shouldn't take long to get what we need."

"Aye. You're right. I'm sure you are."

"I know I am. Now, keep quiet."

Nobi didn't need to hear anymore. Not that they were going to continue talking.

And she certainly didn't need to see any more. Or rather, anything at all. All she could see were the large bushes. She knew enough, and now she really needed to find Chris and talk with him. He would know what to do. She trusted him. With her life. Of that, she could be absolutely certain.

He would help restore the equilibrium. Bring everything back to normal. To a calm state. He would settle her and the situation because that's what he was, a settler.

Well, that was a peculiar way to put it, but the man oozed peace. With him around, there was no chance for chaos to ensue. He was like her solid rock. A firm foundation of safety and peace. See? A settlement.

CHAPTER TWO

CHRIS, DUKE OF Saxby, contemplated the benefits of him having drunk a little more last night. It was a wedding celebration after all. Sally and Jacob said their vows, tears were shed, laughs were had, and he…well, he mostly enjoyed it. It was probably rude to say that he was eager to leave, so he hadn't said it, not to anyone. Hardly even to himself because, truly, he didn't fully understand why he wanted to leave. Sally and Jacob were his friends, and he was happy for them. Overjoyed. Probably.

And besides that, he had been surrounded by friends for the entire house party. He had no reason to be keen on leaving. Yet…he itched for something more. He just couldn't put his finger on it. It was like looking for that perfect place to lay a hat and not being able to find it, so a person just walked around dumbly with a hat outstretched between their fingers. That's how he felt. Like he was holding a hat and he didn't know where to place it. So, the next best place for a hat was just back on a person's head, and that meant said person was heading out.

Chris shook his head, noticing the rambling nature of his thoughts. It was all amounting to the same thing. He needed something new. He needed a change of scenery. He needed to get out of there.

It was for the best. There was no sense in delaying the inevitable. It was like pulling out a tooth, best to just rip it out. He rubbed his jaw at the thought of his younger days. Had he really used a door and a string to pull out a tooth that he was over eager to have gone? Thankfully, he had matured into a much more patient man. At least, most of the time he was quite patient.

Hadn't he just spent all morning looking for Nobi? In doing that, he exerted a tremendous amount of patience. But that was because he absolutely needed to talk with her before he left. Why hadn't they made plans to bid adieu? They weren't the kind to do that. Well…except when they had made plans in the past. Good plans. Marvelous plans. Plans a man dreamt about happening while he waited for them to happen, and then those same plans he dreamt about after they occurred because the real thing was better than his previous dreams.

At the thoughts, warmth flooded Chris in places he didn't want to mention. He locked those thoughts in a box like he always did.

But really, he needed to talk to Nobi. He had been withholding his secret from her for too long. They both knew it was going to happen soon, but he hadn't told her how soon. Chris didn't normally consider himself a careless man, or a man lacking courage…but this last summer (and wasn't that the crux of it?) he had been quieter (less courageous) than usual. At least when it came to Nobi.

They had been spending extra time around each other, he should have been able to tell her his plans. It was easy to tell her because she already knew he wanted to do it…she just didn't know when.

When being now. After this house party he would be leaving.

At the prospect of his adventure, something almost resembling pain lanced through his chest. No, that couldn't be right. It wasn't pain. He was excited. Enthralled. Delirious with anticipation, no? He needed only to imagine the pyramids that he had up until now only seen paintings of. Or he could envision the cathedrals he would walk through with their stained glass windows. And the food…mmm…he was beyond eager to try new foods, have new spices and flavors burst over his tongue.

Yes. That was what he wanted to do, and that's what he was finally going to do. Nothing was going to stop him now. There was no one in his way. No one…at all…

He was finally getting to do what he had always wanted. Ever since he could remember this had been his dream.

Only his friends and family had prevented him from leaving. Not like they were anything significant or anything…

But they hadn't prevented his departure in a naysaying fashion, just their sheer presence (and state of being) had waylaid him.

Why leave when everything was good? Sam, Wes, James, and he were the closest friends; the Betting Buddies. If things were good, there was no point in leaving. But when first Wes found a wife, and then James got engaged, well, Chris started making plans for his own life. There was no point in putting it on hold any longer. Despite that pesky pain ribbing him in his chest.

And it was a good thing, too, that he had put plans into action, because then Sam had gone and married as well.

Of course, all the planning had all been triggered by his father's passing a while ago. But in the moment of his death, Chris had been too grieved to think about himself. He had been taking care of his father for so long, preparing himself (and everyone) for his father's imminent departure, that he just hadn't put as much planning into what would happen for him after his father's death.

Well, that and he respected and honored his father. It wasn't as though he resented being with him up until his death. He had tried to hold onto each moment together. Sharing meals, playing cards after dinner, and talking about anything and everything.

He soaked up as much as his father as he could, knowing he would pass away soon, and then he would have no time to learn about how his father grew up. He wouldn't be able to ask him the first time he rode a horse. (Four years old). The first time he kissed a woman. (Sixteen years old). His favorite homemade meal. (Chicken and potatoes).

So the last few years, after he graduated college, Chris had made sure to be close to home, able to spend time with his father. They had worked meticulously to ensure the estate was in good order and that they had a man of business they could trust. There was no reason for Chris to be worried. They had planned everything down to the last detail. To the point that Chris was hardly needed to manage anything personally. It was all time well spent.

And he would never regret it. He had peace about his decision to postpone his own dreams.

He was a man made of peace. He was a peacekeeper. Peace-maker. Peace-instiller.

So…about this burrowing feeling in his chest…that was new. It was not the peaceful feeling that normally resided within him. Normally he felt settled and calm. His friends looked to him to be the level-headed one in the group, amidst an argument or fight. He wasn't easily riled up. But right now, the ruffling feeling was borderline painful. Certainly beyond irritating. All of it was vexing, and he just didn't have the patience to analyze it further. He needed to talk to Nobi, but she wasn't available. He reassured himself. He would send her a note. They would correspond.

He rubbed his chest, right over his heart. It was fine. Forget the churning sensations.

He chalked it up to nerves, knowing Nobi wouldn't be happy to hear his news. But he felt as though he owed it to her to tell her in person. After all they had been through together. The memories, the various incarnations of her swept through his mind so rapidly he couldn't pick just one to land on. All their firsts together tumbled one over the other, clamoring to gain dominance in his mind's eye. It was all her, together. Each bit and piece. Each memory. All synchronized together to form Nobi. His friend.

And she was a good friend. *Friend*. The word sat awkwardly on his tongue, not wanting to roll off of it.

But that's what she was. They had agreed upon it very clearly. And repeatedly.

So, knowing how to treat a good friend, he was in search of this good friend, to tell her the good news that a good friend would only be too delighted to hear.

He was finally going to be the world traveler he had always dreamed of becoming. Adventure awaited. And he could feel the anticipation roiling through him. There was no one particular destination. No one place he wanted to settle. He wasn't a settler. He wanted to roam. Be free. Explore.

He had traversed England as much as he could without going too far from home. Now he wanted to venture onto the continent. He envied those who had explored caves and partaken in archeological digs. Not because he wanted to find anything, but simply for the experience. He wanted to breathe new air, taste new food, and see new sites. And he didn't plan to stop on the continent. It was his dream to venture as far as India and China. Perhaps further if he could. There were no constraints now. Well, not really.

He could explore the open roads, the wide open skies, the vast emptiness that lay before him. Emptiness for him to fill. Nothing was stopping him from going. So long as one didn't count that one friend. Which he couldn't. She would marry soon, and their friendship was bound to change dramatically at that time anyway. Despite the wince that permeated his stomach, he'd rather put distance between them when that time came. He didn't especially envy the idea of watching her walk down the aisle, so it was best to send his felicitations from afar.

They could still be friends. Of course.

But at this juncture in his life, he didn't want to feel guilty about pursuing his dreams.

So much time had been spent sacrificing (and yes, it had been rewarding), but now he wanted to live life for himself. A life worthy of his soul.

And that soul was calling out to him to find more. Yes, he could hear her calling and he was desperate to answer that one word on repeat. Adventure.

— ❦ —

CHAPTER THREE

Six Years Ago

IT WAS HER debut season. She should be thrilled to be out. She should be thrilled at the attention some men were paying to her. Asking her to dance, asking to get her a lemonade (though she preferred sherry), asking her name, and sometimes, if she were lucky, sometimes they even asked about her hobbies or interests. Well, that had happened one time, and it might have just been a segue into him wanting to share his interest in studying spiders. Fair enough, everyone should have a hobby they loved, but when he mentioned that he could show her his findings, well, at that point, the dance was over before it really began, wasn't it?

And there was that other gentleman, the one who had asked her about paintings. And art, well, that sounded like a lovely topic to discuss. How delightful. Though she didn't know much more than the average lady on painting, colors, and various techniques, she still welcomed the topic. But then he had asked (a little too eagerly) whether she had seen the private collection the host had in residence. He seemed a little too keen on implying the forbidden nature of the collection. So of course that dance would never be turning into a second one...not on this night or any other in the future.

The ballrooms should still captivate her, enthrall her though. There were other men. Plenty of men not interested in spiders or scandalous paintings, surely she could find one. Just one. That's all it took. But the men, the glitter, the shimmering candles, the intoxicating fragrance from the abundance of flowers…it was all a bit…cloying. She should be enjoying it, but there were so many shoulds that Nobi wanted to escape them for a bit.

She could pretend to be a proper lady all the time…or…she could just go be by herself and regroup before putting on a face again.

She didn't even mind putting on a face all that much. There was a reason for it. It made for seamless conversations, effortless introductions, and graceful dancing. And those were all worthwhile endeavors in high society. She liked them…she really did. But they were all falling a bit flat.

A quick step out into the gardens, under the darkness of night, with a breath of fresh air, and she would be as good as new.

Nobi picked up her hem and raced down the steps, casting a glance around, she ducked down further into the garden where there were fewer and fewer candles lighting the path.

With a deep inhale she rested her back against the trunk of a tree and dropped her head back to gaze out from under the branches at the night sky. The stars twinkled a wave from their distance. She blinked a wave back and closed her eyes.

Her chest relaxed as her hands rubbed mindlessly against a soft patch of fabric on her skirts.

This was what she needed. Just a moment to breathe.

CRUNCH. CRUNCH. CRUNCH.

Leaves underfoot, their existence crumbling at a sharp pace, and her eyes flickered open. Heavy breaths. Manly breaths. How did she know that? She didn't know how she knew, she just did. She could feel it in her bones.

Nobi's fingers curled against her skirts and she transferred the weight of her body from her heels to her toes.

There was a man ducking under her tree. Yes, it was her tree now. Couldn't he see that? Oh…perhaps he couldn't see her at all. Dash it! That had been the point in hiding outside, but really, now, she was in for it. She knew what it meant to be found alone with a man. Scandal. And if not scandal, it could be dangerous.

She didn't know the man...but she had been told that men took things from women they shouldn't.

Though she wasn't quite certain of all the details, enough of the fear of God had been instilled within her that her blood was running quite cold at the moment. The man was breathing heavily, as if he had been running away from something. She could obviously offer him no protection.

Perhaps if she stood perfectly still, he would just move along. *Be the tree. He can't see you.* He was just on the other side of the tree trunk, if only he would just stay there.

But of course he didn't. The second he fumbled around the truck, he bumped into her.

"Yipes!" Quite the unmanly sound escaped from his broad silhouette.

And the sound so shocked her that she didn't have the wherewithal to be afraid; instead, she giggled.

"Oh, a man's suffering is your pleasure, is it?" the voice asked archly.

In a low voice, so as not to disturb the stillness of the night, she answered, "Not usually. But I don't think I've ever heard a man utter such a word in such a fashion." The last few words stuttered out on a second giggle.

"You find this all quite amusing then? My manliness in shreds?" She couldn't see his eyes in the shadows, but somehow she could just imagine them twinkling like the stars above.

"It's rather funny, I must admit."

"I'm glad you think so—" and in a trice his hand was over her mouth, and his body had stepped closer. Her mind whirled and thoughts shook like the leaves in the tree. In a windstorm. Had she read him all wrong? What was he doing? Why was he so close to—

"Sh..." his breath was warm on her neck. In fact, his body was warm all over her. "There's a woman after me."

Unable to express herself, she raised her eyebrows, hoping he would notice.

"She's relentless in trying to trap me into marriage." He leaned his forehead against hers, intimately. Yet…comfortingly. Well, more so for him. It seemed almost as though he were trying to draw comfort from her…

She must have wiggled because he pulled back. "Don't move. I don't want her to find me. Or us for that matter." And then he stepped back another half step, and perhaps having realized the fright he might have caused her, he removed his hand. "God, I'm sorry. I don't know what I was thinking—"

"Duke?" A female voice singsonged a whisper into the air.

And Nobi's heart wrenched within her. She knew about obligations and expectations. No one should be forced into anything. If the man didn't want to marry the relentless husband-hunter out there in the dark, he shouldn't have to. What kind of woman trapped a man into marriage anyway?

She couldn't offer this man protection, yet, in a way she could. There wasn't a moment to lose. She had no time to reconsider her decision. Besides, the words just plopped out without her consent.

"Pretend you're with me," she whispered. And her hands. Damn those normally subservient hands. They reached out and grabbed his jacket pulling him closer.

"If you want my protection, pretend you're with me." She said it again. At his bewilderment, she loosened her grip. The moment was gone. Shattered. His twinkling eyes, the warmth of his body, she had been caught up in them for God knows what reason, and she had acted the ultimate addle-pated idiot.

But then one of his hands covered hers, and one flew to the tree trunk. And his face was inches—no, just one single inch—from hers. And his eyes were amused. Intense. Cautious. As though he were trying to decipher the meaning of a joke.

"All right. But I'll be the gentleman. You needn't fear me. I won't touch you, and I won't let her see you." He pressed even closer to her, and she could tell that he was trying to hide her face but not her skirts. Protect her. "If she thinks I'm out here with another woman, she'll run back inside."

With the thickness of her tongue, and the dryness of her throat, Nobi could only nod.

When his lips grazed her ear, saying, "I think she's almost here. She'll see me soon enough," she gasped. Loudly. And it was one of those gasps that hummed into the air.

And her gasp must have pulled the trigger on the relentless woman, because the husband-hunter too gasped. And her stomps could be heard all the way back to the ballroom.

"That was perfect," the man mumbled into her ear.

He was still pressed up against her, despite the woman's hightailing it out of the darkness.

"Was it?" Nobi asked, unsure of what her next move should be.

"It was. And there's no way she would be able to identify you. Not with the shadows we're in. You saved me." Her hands were splayed out against his chest (when had that happened?), and she felt a soft laugh rumble out of him when he kissed her temple. "I owe you...my life."

Ah...yes. Her first kiss. Sealed with a promise. Her insides had turned gooey. Her toes were curling, seeking to dig tunnels in the ground beneath her slippers.

This man, this nameless man, was handsome. Playful. Honorable. And he wanted to live life on his own terms, not at the demands of someone else. He was...perfect.

She sighed.

He stepped back. "God, I'm sorry. I keep crowding you. I came out here to escape the crowd for a moment, and here I am...doing...what?" He rubbed his fingers along his jaw, which she could make out had just the slightest amount of stubble on it. "What are we doing here, Lady...?"

"Lady Zenobia. Or just, Nobi."

"Nobi." Her name sounded how velvet felt, soft, warm, and like she wanted to rub herself all over the way he spoke. That made no sense.

Dash it! What was she thinking? She needed to get ahold of herself.

"I'm Chris." He cleared his throat, and mumbled, "Duke of Saxby, one-day-to-be. I guess you should know. No use hiding it."

"Oh. So that's why she was after you?"

"Now wait a second. Are you saying she was only after my dukedom?"

Dash it! She needed to retract her statement. Or was it an assumption? "Oh dear. I'm sorry, I didn't mean to insult—"

His laughter rippled through her ramblings.

"I'm joking. Of course that's all she was after. What she knows about me amounts to a grand total of two things. She can match my title to my face."

"I'm glad I didn't offend you."

"It's hard to offend me."

"That's…good to know." And somehow she felt like she had been given a small peek into his inner workings. Already, she knew more about him than the husband-hunter. She knew his title, his face, and that he was not easily offended. Hmm…that did make her wonder…

"What would it take to offend you?"

Chris rubbed his jaw again. "Not sure I should give a woman that kind of ammunition."

"I'm not just any woman—"

"You know, before you finish that thought. I already regret saying it." He shook his head. "To evince you of my contrition, I'll tell you two things that would offend me. One, if you called into question my honor. And two, if you insulted my family."

And wonder of wonders, warmth spread through her body again. And he hadn't stepped any closer to her. Just learning his depths produced a melting effect within her.

"I would never…"

"I didn't think you would."

"How would you know? You don't know me," she said lightly.

"You know,"—he rubbed his jaw for a third time—"it's true, I don't really know you at all. Yet, I feel like I might."

"How's that?" Her curiosity was piqued now. How could a man feel as though he knew a woman in only an instant?

"You're loyal. Protective. Compassionate. Caring. Considering what you just did for me. I'd say there's not much you wouldn't do for your family or those closest to you." All true. She supposed it was possible for a man to read a woman in an instant. Not fully, of course, but at least accurately.

He wasn't done. "I'd say more, but as a gentleman, I really shouldn't."

But those things he didn't want to say…for some reason, the sizzling sensation within her told her that those were the things she really wanted to hear.

"What shouldn't you say?"

And then he turned those twinkling eyes on her, but instead of the shimmering light, she saw the black of night. An intensity. A depth. A vastness she couldn't fathom in only one glance.

"Let's just say," and his voice dropped into a husky rasp, "you're as beautiful on the outside as you are on the inside."

A bullet zinged straight to her heart. And her heart was leaking something it shouldn't. Because, well, a heart shouldn't leak at all. But she couldn't stop it. She was feeling all kinds of things for a man she didn't know. This way led to danger. But it didn't feel dangerous. It felt safe. It felt like he would never be the type of man to hurt her. That he would put her needs above his own. It felt as though given the choice between her wellbeing and his own, he would sacrifice himself for her. But how could she read that about him in such a few short moments? It was madness to feel such a connection with him so quickly. As though she knew him. Not even that. It was more that she had always known him but didn't know where he was. She had been searching and now she had found him. How…odd.

And even odder, at the point of finding each other, it felt like they were mutually, instinctively agreed upon protecting each other. What the dickens was that about? It couldn't be real, could it?

CHAPTER FOUR

NOBI WAS RATTLED, so perhaps it wasn't the best line of conversation to pursue, but her curiosity couldn't be assuaged.

"Who was the woman hunting you down?"

At Chris's widened eyes, she momentarily thought she had overstepped. And of course, she had. She didn't know this man, and prying into his personal affairs was akin to asking him to undress before her. Not that she would ever ask him to do that for her. But the thought of it sent a flush of heat up her neck. She could only hope he didn't see it in the darkness.

"I-I am sorry. I shouldn't have asked—"

"It's quite all right. There's really no harm in discussing it. You would probably recognize her back in the ballroom anyway."

But she didn't correct him. Really, there was no point in telling him that she had been too overstimulated by the heat of his body and his fresh soap scent to take a look at a random woman lurking in the gardens. No. She would definitely never admit that to him.

He rubbed the back of his neck before continuing. "That was Lady Evelyn."

And she wanted to wait in the silence. Let him provide further information only if he wanted to…but—

"Has she been pursuing you for a long time now?" popped out instead to burst the small bubble of silence.

A throaty chuckle emerged from his lips, sending tingles down her spine. "Let's just say that it's been a while longer than I'd like it to be."

"Have you taken any measures against her?"

His cocked eyebrow urged her to explain.

"Perhaps you could…"—and even though she knew it was a terrible idea, she threw it out into the universe anyway—"fake a relationship? You've already faked a tryst." More warmth soaked into her cheeks. She wasn't sure how much more heat they could bear. They were about to burst into flames on the spot.

"Are you offering yourself for the position?"

Oh. And that was it. Her hands flew to her cheeks. If she didn't do it, she was sure they would combust. "I-I…oh—"

Another rumble of laughter swept through him. "Ah, dear Nobi. You are good for the soul." He brushed his hand along her shoulder. "Don't worry. I'm not asking. I wouldn't put you through that. Can you imagine how complicated that would be?"

Yes. She could imagine all the complications. Feigning attraction. Spending too much time with him. Feeling the pull of his body. It would, undoubtedly, be the simple, most complicated task she could attempt to take on in her lifetime.

"It would be complicated," she offered. And then, because apparently she had no filter this evening, she added, "But I would do it. For you."

His hand landed on her shoulder again with a light squeeze. "You know, Nobi, I believe you would do that."

Something crackled in the air between them. It was like she was trying to see the fire but was only able to hear it.

And then, perhaps because he wanted to avoid being singed by any of the sparks flying, or perhaps (sadly) he didn't notice any of them, he said, "Let's just hope she finds another duke to hunt."

And because Nobi wouldn't have known what to do about wayward sparks, she simply agreed. "Yes. It's a wonder that any women do that. I can't imagine ever trying to snare a duke."

"You wouldn't have to," she thought she heard him say. But

he was plodding on. "Some women have goals in life. Whether due to personal values, societal pressure, or financial afflictions. You never know what life may bring."

She hoped it would never bring her to that point of desperation.

"Look at this ball, for instance. Would you ever think you might live to be one hundred?"

"Oh, is that what we're celebrating this evening?"

"You didn't notice the signage? Hear the toast?"

She giggled at her cluelessness. "I must admit I've been a touch less observant than I normally am. All the balls are merging into one giant event of which I'll have one memory." Except this one. After having met Chris, she knew this ball would stand out.

"It's actually my grandfather's birthday."

"My stars! I should let you return to the festivities."

"Please," his hand moved to her shoulder again and slid down her forearm, "don't go. My family understands my need to slip away on occasion."

"All right." She swallowed. She could see herself settling down with a man like him. Or him…exactly. "If you're sure you won't be missed."

"Only by Lady Evelyn. She's probably already devising plans for me though."

"To snag you or to make a doll of you to stick pins in?"

"My, my, my, Nobi. Is there a dark side to you?"

She shook her head playfully as her lip curled up into a smile. "I would never do that. But Lady Evelyn seems like that type."

Vibrations of laughter rippled through the air. "She does seem the type, doesn't she?" After the laughter settled, filling the air with mirth, he said, "My grandfather almost got caught in scandal. But thankfully he found the love of his life, my grandmother. They were married after only meeting one time. He knew the instant he met her that they were destined to be together."

"That's lovely."

"Yes. It took him a while to find her, but once they did, they never looked back."

"It sounds like you have a very loving family."

"My grandfather is a great man. He has lived a full life, and I can only hope to live a life half as honorable as him."

She could see the admiration in his eyes, but she also sensed a touch of melancholia. "Are you worried for him?"

"I wouldn't say worried." He shook his head, stopping the flow of his admission. "This is too much to be sharing with a stranger, isn't it?"

"Sometimes it's nice to open up to someone who doesn't know you. It's a fresh start."

He hummed his agreement. "Well, in that case, I wouldn't say I'm worried. I would just say that I'm not sure how my father is feeling. To see his father growing older. Taking over the dukedom. And then one day that will be me." He scrubbed a hand down his face. "It's a lot to think about."

"You have time to prepare for it."

"I know that to be truer than anyone else. It's all my life is about. Preparing to be a duke."

"On that front we are similar."

"How so?"

"All my life is about preparing to be a lady and find a husband."

"It's a wonder you're not on the prowl for a duke. You aren't, are you?" he waggled his eyebrows.

"I assure you, I am not. A duke…is a bit…reaching for me."

"I don't think so."

"What kind of duchess would I make, if someone were to find me hiding out while hosting my own balls?"

"The same kind of duke I'll make *when* I hide during the balls my duchess hosts."

And Nobi could see it. It was a brightly painted picture of her being a duchess, to him. But she had no right to dream that big. She should end this wishful thinking now before her heart dared to hope too much. Before her heart soaked up too much of him that it would be impossible to wring him out of her system.

"Well, I should go back inside before someone notices my absence."

His face fell, and she thought perhaps he might be a bit disappointed. If he felt anything for her, she wanted to let that hope take root.

"Is there anything I can do to entice you to stay?" he asked.

Yes. There were several things she could think of, but none she could voice. Her stomach decided to speak for her with a growl. Her hands flew to her face in mortification.

Between her fingers, she mumbled, "I should go inside to eat."

"Wait." He held her in place with his hands on her hips. And if that didn't light a fire on the spot and blaze down between her legs. "Let me grab us a snack. Give me a few more minutes before we go back and face the crowds."

She couldn't have gone inside if she wanted to. The internal inferno building inside of her was quite possibly externally visible now. So she simply nodded, needing the time to understand the heated liquid pooling between her thighs.

She watched, rooted in the spot, as he rushed away.

Earlier, all she had wanted to do was escape the crush for a few minutes to catch her breath. Little did she know she would find herself anchored to a tree, nearly anchored to a man, and never wanting to return so long as this man was with her.

She had never believed in love at first sight before. But the thought of it now made her lightheaded. It couldn't be possible to find someone so perfect. He must have a flaw.

Within minutes, Chris was jaunting back to her with a wide grin on his face and hands casually clasped at his sides.

"I grabbed what I could, but I didn't want to make a scene. So I had to take what was on the first tray. I tucked them into my palms." he chuckled. "Hopefully no one noticed."

He was so sweet, giddy like a little boy who had just stolen cookies from the kitchen. Or snagged a second dessert from the cook before going to bed. With his dark sandy hair and blue eyes, she was sure he was not one to be denied. Especially if he put one of his charming grins on his face.

His palms were out in front of her. "Which one do you want?" His face screwed up in a tight knot before laughing. "Yipes! You probably want neither of these."

The treats were mangled, smashed, wilted...altogether not a shape a dessert would normally take.

And she had to giggle at how adorable he was to even bring a treat to her.

"I'll take that one," she said and pointed to his left hand unsure of what was in it. But it looked creamy.

She reached for it, but before she could grab it, he whispered, "Wait." Then he shoved his right palm in his mouth, devouring the first dessert. Smatters of custard landed around his lips. She almost brushed the crumbs away, but it was far too intimate a gesture for her to feel comfortable doing it. Surely he would wipe his own face. And he did...only...he missed a spot.

Before she could point it out, he stepped closer to her, "Let me."

"Oh...um...what? Why?"

"It's very messy. I don't want you to get your hands dirty."

Her eyes widened as he lifted a portion of the treat to her mouth. But she was incapable of doing anything other than being submissive to his kind control. Involuntarily, her mouth opened. And God, his fingers were brushing against her lips, the corner of her mouth. Then he placed the most decadent dessert in all of England on her tongue. And she couldn't stop from closing her eyes and letting out a soft moan.

She let herself savor the soft texture. The sweet flavor. The moment. With him.

When he cleared his throat, she hadn't realized her eyes were still closed until they flew open to catch him studying her.

"Do you like it?" The intensity of his eyes burned into her, searing a path to her heart.

She nodded and her tongue darted out along her bottom lip. She thought she caught a sound coming from him, but she wasn't sure. And then the last bite was placed before her. She opened her mouth and he placed the bite inside. His finger lingered at the corner of her mouth and she could taste him. She wanted more. Her heart was pounding so hard she was sure it was going to flop right out of her chest.

And then he took his treat-encased fingers and slid them into his own mouth, licking off the rest of the dessert.

Her head felt light. Her knees buckled.

"Nobi?" His arm latched around her waist. "Are you all right? We should get you inside. Perhaps you need more than a little petit four."

"I'm fine," she murmured, though she was the furthest thing from it. He was a god among men. Her heart, her mind, her soul, her entire *body* could feel it. It was thrumming through her, louder, longer, heavier, than any musical note had ever rung.

She should say something. But what would he think of her? After all they had discussed about snagging a duke. She couldn't' say anything. About her feelings at least. So she kept it safe.

She grasped onto something in reality instead. The first thing that came to mind, she blurted out. "Petit four? Little cakes? That sounds French."

"Yes. They're little French desserts. I can't wait to travel there one day and try them. In fact, I plan on traveling the world one day and trying as many desserts as I can from every country. Beyond desserts, of course, I'll visit museums, the pyramids, cathedrals, the theater. I want the adventure…" his excitement trailed on.

And there it was. The flaw. He was a restless soul, looking to flit from place to place. He wanted adventure. She wanted to settle. There was no future there. She knew how that kind of soul lived. And she wanted nothing to do with it.

"I think I had better go inside." Her legs were wobbly again, for an entirely new reason.

"Are you going to faint?"

"No. I'm fine."

"I can find some smelling salts, if you're going to swoon."

His kindness was a stab of pain inside her. Twisting. Relentless.

Besides, she needed something a whole lot stronger than smelling salts to wake up from this sudden darkness.

CHAPTER FIVE

Present Day

CHRIS WAS ALMOST out the door when a premonition struck him. He really couldn't leave without saying goodbye to Nobi. It felt wrong. Like the sky would shake an angry fist at him in the form of hail if he went against etiquette. Etiquette? His heart was laughing at him, but he didn't hear it for it was. Regardless, he accepted that it wasn't etiquette pulling him back into the house.

He turned around and came face to face with Jacob, the new groom, who shouldn't be down here. "Oh, Jacob. I'm glad I ran into you, though I didn't expect to see you this morning."

His ear tips rimmed in red as he murmured, "Just…erm…grabbing a few…flowers." He coughed roughly. "For Sally,"—he scratched his head awkwardly before adding— "to smell."

Chris cleared his throat. Well, that was unnecessary information. And also a prevarication if he ever heard one. Anyway, he didn't really want to know what Jacob was going to do with flowers on Sally's body. Before Jacob could take off though, he needed to get to the point.

"I was just about to leave but I realized I didn't have a chance to say goodbye to Zenobia yet. Have you seen her around this morning? I'm sure that's a silly question."

"Actually, Sally inquired about Zenobia to find out when she was leaving and Zenobia told her that she was going to sneak in some target practice before she left. So I'm sure she's there."

"All right. Thank you."

"Glad to help. Now, erm…I'm just going to go grab those flowers."

"Sure." Chris nodded with a dim smile. And Jacob almost took off again before Chris remembered his manners. "That was a great house party, Jacob. I wish you and Sally marital bliss."

In reply, Jacob only blushed further into his cheeks, waved, and slipped into the garden.

Perfect. Nobi was out gallivanting about the property. He really didn't want to go find her now. She would be all wind-blown, with a flush in her cheeks. And she would be happy, doing what she loved. He didn't want to disturb that.

Feet firmly planted shoulder width apart, he could feel the push and the pull—first one way and then the other.

Push. He should go. She was his friend, and he needed to talk to her. Pull. This shouldn't be such a difficult decision. He didn't feel this guilt—yes, he supposed that's what it was—to bid adieu to everyone else at the party. Push. But it was Zenobia…she was different.

Pull. It didn't matter.

The decision was simple. He would see her back at home. He wiped his hands together as if settling the matter physically would ease the emotional turmoil.

So, against the knots forming in the pit of his stomach, he leapt up into the waiting carriage and took off.

The rumbling wheels of the carriage against the dirt road matched the rocks bumbling around inside of him, and he didn't get more than fifteen minutes away before he changed his mind. He had to return and say goodbye. He had to tell her about his plans. It couldn't wait.

Banging on the roof of the carriage, Chris called out, "Stop the horses."

He knew he was being foolish, but sometimes a man needed to listen to his gut. He would take one of the horses back, tell her the news, and then be on his way home.

He reached to open the door when he heard a peculiar sound. A thunk followed by a grunt and another thud.

Perhaps the driver was having a bit of trouble reigning in one of the horses. But those sounds didn't quite match the scenario he was playing in his head. No matter, he would find out in a second what was going on.

The door squeaked open, the sunlight hitting his eyes and momentarily blinding him. It took a second for him to find his footing and jump down.

But instead of being greeted by the open road, or the driver, a gruff voice sounded in his ears. And then he knew. This was the storm, the clouds, the discolored sky that his gut had been warning him about. This was the premonition being fulfilled. But he didn't have time to react or find his bearings. His mind was on his regrets. On Zenobia. And that blinding sun. He still couldn't make out any figures in front of him. Just a silhouette, and it didn't look friendly. In fact, it looked very unfriendly. And he couldn't tell, but was that a gun?

"'Bout time you showed up. We've been waiting for you."

What the—

Blackness enveloped him as he slumped to the ground.

God…his head ached. How long had he been out? His tongue pushed roughly against some fabric. Great. Gagged. His hands immediately made an attempt to remove the gag, but they were bound behind his back.

"The duke's awake," a skinny bloke nudged a burlier man beside him. The larger of the two had been staring out the window, and Chris could see a pistol on his lap.

His head hurt like hell and his heart was stampeding in his chest. He needed to get out of here. He needed to see Zenobia. What the hell had he been thinking? He should have listened to his gut. He could kick himself right now. Which…really was about all he could do since thankfully his legs weren't tied up.

Instinctively, he wanted to know why these two ruffians had abducted him. Sure, he was a duke, and they could be using him for ransom. But surely there were older, more feeble dukes that would serve an easier target. Chris wasn't a particularly prideful man. Certainly, no one would admonish him for his conceit. But really, he was a strapping, young (enough) duke that he wouldn't have been someone's first pick as an easy target.

So, with some pride (and he hoped, more logic), he had to presume the men were after something else.

His head wasn't quite clear from the blow though, and it was a touch difficult to sift through possible reasons for being abducted. His two closest friends had recently wed. One had been well on their way to the chapel...But those were the most significant goings on in his life...except...

Only one thing stood out. Sam had entrusted him with a package before the house party started. But these ruffians couldn't possibly know about that. No one knew about it. It had only been Sam and Chris who were privy to that exchange. And well, of course one couldn't discount two households full of servants. But their servants were loyal to them. Weren't they?

Chris started to make a mental list of all the people he employed, but he wasn't able to get far through his list, as he was interrupted by nature. Or, nature's call to be more precise.

"I gotta take a piss," one of the ruffians announced with a grumble.

"Hold it," the larger of the two answered without making eye contact with his cohort. "We're almost there."

"I can't hold it. Been waiting too long."

"Bloody hell, Lester. We were waiting in the bushes all morning. You didn't think to go then?"

"What can I tell you, Jax—I thought we weren't using our names—I have to go. Now." The skinny fellow started rubbing the cushion with his bottom, doing an awkward dance on the seat. A dance that Chris would never be able to erase from his memory.

"So unless you want this carriage to stink like—"

"Stop!" Jax bellowed. "Get out." He thrust the door open and

Lester tumbled over Jax's lap.

Chris didn't have time to think, never mind plan his escape. He saw the moment for what it was and exploited it.

Lester was still crawling over Jax's lap, for God knows what reason, and Chris was only too grateful to the divine for their stupidity. He inched toward the other door while Jax snarled at his friend. "Get your cock off my leg, you sodding fool. Take your piss—"

"Ahh!" Lester toppled onto the dirt floor and Jax moved to take a step out of the carriage to help his friend.

Chris shoved his shoulder against the other door, praying it was unlocked. It was. He tumbled down to the ground, but he didn't give himself a second to consider what new bruises he might have added to his body. Propping himself up on his knees, he pushed up to a squat, and then shot himself up to standing. He took off running. The trees were close to the road. He dove into them, desperate for cover.

He could hear the two still arguing at the carriage but kept running.

He didn't stop when he heard Jax demand, "Lester, put your cock back in your pants. Let's go."

When they yelled out, "Duke! Get back here!" He ran faster. His body was weak, his legs were drained. But his heart was strong. He had motivation on his side. He had hope on his side. He had love—

WHUMP!

A harsh forest floor. Green grass. Flowers. A thick tree trunk. Those were a beautiful sight. So many memories. One in particular. What a night to remember. If he had to choose a memory to play in his mind before going down, this would definitely be one of them. In fact, it was probably playing front and center right now due to how often he recalled it at night before he went to sleep. Innocent. Pleasure. Her.

His vision blurred as layers of glass kept presenting themselves atop his eyes. It wasn't meant to be this way. He needed to tell her...

Blackness.

And later, for the second time that day, in what was really far too close to the previous bout of unconsciousness, Chris woke up.

If he had thought his head ached before, he was quite sure it had split right down the middle this time. It was like lifting a horse with a pinky to pry his eyes open. His head sagged back against the squabs.

Incidentally, it was a good thing he didn't want to kick himself for trying to escape, because this time he couldn't even do that if he wanted to. His legs were bound tightly at the ankles.

Not normally one to show weakness, he didn't care right this second. He released a groan. Now his body throbbed, and he was furious. He grumbled against the gag until Lester pulled it out of his mouth.

"What are you saying, Duke?"

"What do you want with me?"

"All that will be coming in good time. Don't worry. When we get there, we'll explain everything—oomph!" Lester rubbed his side where Jax had blasted him with an elbow. "Aye. Not everything. Just the things you need to know."

Even if he wanted to, Chris didn't have the energy to pursue that line of questioning. His eyes slammed shut and he couldn't hold his head up any longer. This time, unlike the previous two, he succumbed to darkness of his own volition and let his body sleep. He would need his energy when he woke up, because there was no way he was going out like this. If all he did was see Nobi one last time, he could die happy. Or at least, happy enough.

CHAPTER SIX

Six Years Ago

THE VERY FIRST night Chris had ever met Nobi, stuck out in his mind like an elephant walking down Bond Street. He never would have expected to meet her under a tree in the middle of a garden in the dark of night. No one could have predicted that encounter. And the way she had been cautious and meek, yet self-assured, wrapped itself around his heart.

She was quieter, he could tell because he was the same way. Hence them both sneaking out of a party. But she knew who she was and she was happy with herself. And something about her drew him in. When Lady Evelyn had come looking for him, he couldn't have thought of a better husband-hunting deterrent than to lose himself in Nobi's arms.

He would never forget the way she had looked up at him in earnest, vouching to be his fake tryst for a few minutes. She trusted him implicitly, and his heart had swelled. To be held in such high regard so quickly by a woman who otherwise seemed so reserved, was humbling. He was drawn to her, that was certain.

And he hardly even knew her.

That's just how it was sometimes. There were those times you could meet a person and you felt as though you could read their soul. You understood their motivation in life. You matched dispositions…or if not matched, complemented. He felt all of that with Zenobia within minutes of meeting her. As though there was an invisible string tethering their souls.

But then she had scurried off, just when he thought that everything was going really well. He must have misread her entirely. Or perhaps it had been one-sided. He couldn't believe it, given the gravity of his feelings, but he was not so obnoxious or short sighted to consider that the effects had all been on his side. If it was only him, he had to respect that.

And being as he was not one to force things in life, he didn't intentionally seek her out after that night. If she wanted his attention, she would have made it clear on the first night. She was not one to prevaricate. Or equivocate. She would articulate. Most definitely.

Within that same week though, he found himself at another ball, in another garden, awkwardly wondering if he might—perchance—run into her again. Not that he was about to admit that he had been lurking (no, not lurking, surveying) the gardens with a little more deliberation of late. To no avail until this night.

And if the first night had been fate, the second night was divine.

Chris found himself taking a small walk around the pond when he came upon her.

She hadn't noticed him yet, so he took his time observing her, as much as he could see beneath the moonlight. Her slippers and stockings were off, and her feet were dangling in the water. Her skirts had been pulled up so that he could see the glimmer of her ankles and part way up her shins. It was not intentionally seductive. It was pure innocent pleasure, and it tugged on his heart.

She was wiggling her feet, as if moving them to a playful dance. Her eyes were watching her toes, or perhaps the reflection of the moon on the water. When her toes stopped tapping against the water, she rested her head back and looked to be studying the stars. He could hear her humming a soft tune.

She resonated peace. In fact, she was the very epitome of contentment. She needed nothing more than the soft shimmer of the moon and the chill of the water to rest her feet in order to find delight.

He didn't want to frighten her, so he made a soft bird call. When she turned her head up into the trees looking for the source of the sound, he cleared his throat softly.

"Well, hello Lady Zenobia." He hadn't quite shaken out the huskiness in his throat when he voiced the words. "We find each other again."

And though he couldn't see it precisely, he had a knowing sensation that her eyes lit up at the sight of him.

That was a good sign.

"Good evening, Duke."

"So formal. After all we've been through." At the quirk of her brow, he insisted on listing the singular event that led to the depth of their relationship. "Our *tryst* and our midnight treat have surely made it suitable for us to refer to each other by our Christian names, Nobi."

Her smile in return lifted his spirits. Without realizing the constriction that had been placed upon himself, he now felt as though he could breathe deeper. Had his lungs increased in size? Or had his chest just found more freedom to expand? The sense of freedom was clear.

She still hadn't said more than three words to him, but he attributed that to the stillness of the night rather than a reluctance toward his company.

"May I join you?"

With two quick taps, she patted the ground beside her. "It's a little bit damp in some spots." And only then did he notice how far up her skirts were bunched so that her bare bottom was sitting on the grass. Her legs were covered, there was nothing noticeably indecent about her posture, but knowing that her legs and bum were exposed sent a shiver through his spine. His swallowing thickened until he set himself down beside her and focused on her face.

And the pond.

But mostly her face.

And those lush, pouty lips.

He had to flicker his attention between the pond and her face, lest he misread something in her soft gray eyes. He had never seen such a color before. And so far, he had only observed them at night. Yet they held a fierce devotion in them. Not to him. Not yet, at least. He would never be so sanguine as to think a woman (like her no less) could fall that hard and that quickly for him. But that gray…some might think the gray likened the clouds, an overcast day, shutting out the sun. But there was no coverage at all. She appeared to be an open book, or at least, a book willing to be opened.

That was a more apt description. She was willing.

And that gray…no, it wasn't like the clouds so much as it was like the metal of a bullet. Powerful but quiet, explosive only if triggered.

He wanted to tell her how he felt about her, but it was far too early to mention anything. Not only that, when he considered how the first night ended, he didn't want to say anything too directly. There was no point in scaring her off. So he decided to bide his time and gauge her body language as well as the conversation.

"Why did you leave the party?" she asked innocently. Only, it wasn't that innocent of an answer. Obviously he needed to deflect the question because he wasn't going to jump into a long winded reply about how he had been keeping an eye out for her at parties, trying to get her alone again. Especially since in getting her alone his foremost intention was conversation. Did that make him sound like a lost puppy trailing behind her? He didn't rightly care.

Though he could have paid her a call. Brought flowers. Invited her on a carriage ride. Spoken to her family. It's what men did when they wanted to state their intentions. But…it seemed too formal. He didn't want to state his intentions, hopefully that didn't sound dishonorable. He just wanted to get to know her under watchless eyes. Like those of the moon.

So no, he didn't say anything except a truth that had nothing to do with his feelings, "I like the night air."

"Me too."

A soft breeze whispered across her cheek. He watched and felt it collecting her loose strands, tumbling them together, and letting them scatter around her face.

She was the most beautiful woman he had ever seen. But it was more than her night black hair and soft gray eyes, it was something emitted by her soul. He wanted to know her more. As much as one human could know another.

"Tell me something about yourself, Nobi." He was leaning back, admiring the view which included the pond but mostly consisted of Nobi. Their hands were both resting behind them, propping their bodies up at an angle. His fingers were inches from hers. He could reach out slightly and touch her if he dared.

He didn't. But he could. And that was comforting in a strange sense.

She gave him a side eye and then flickered her eyes back to the pond. With a soft breath, she expelled some of her reserve and started to share. "I'm the second daughter in a family of four girls. The eldest, Boudicca is a prim spinster and a fencing master. Though I doubt she'll be a spinster forever. Joan is quiet and reserved, and she's a bladesmith. I think she wants to make a business of it, and I know if she wants it, it'll happen because she's incredible. Artemisia is the youngest. She's an archer who is wildly expressive and wants to live a fantasy. I hope she gets everything her heart desires. And I don't just hope for it, I'll do everything in my power to see it happen."

In saying all of that about other people, Nobi disclosed more about herself than Chris thought. She was selfless. Always considering other people. She had the heart of a servant, a nurturer. She was loyal to her family, beyond all else. But still, he wanted to know more. Even though he felt her essence, he wanted her to tell him who she was. He wanted her to trust him.

"What about you?" he prodded. And finally, he reached his

finger over that one inch to tap the top of her finger as he asked. A warmth flooded him from the touch as he recalled holding her close once before. He longed to hold her again. Even just that inch of her finger was smooth and beckoning to him.

"Me?" Genuine surprise marked her features. "I just told you about myself."

"In a roundabout way you did. You told me about your siblings, who they are and what they like to do. But what about you? How would you describe yourself? What do you like to do?"

"I don't often think about describing myself." Her eyes ventured up to the night sky and then settled back down on his face. He thought her eyes dipped to his mouth, but then they were on his eyes with a twinkle in them. "But I can tell you a secret."

And he desperately wanted to know all of her secrets. "Tell me."

"I'm very good at shooting a pistol."

He huffed out a small burst of air in shock. "That—well, that I was not expecting you to say."

Her light giggle landed on his heart. "That's the point of a secret, isn't it?"

"True. The surprise of you shooting a pistol is shocking enough, and I'm grateful you shared that secret with me. It's not shocking to me because I reserve that activity for men, just to be clear. I'm oddly proud that you partake in such an activity. If a woman wants to do something, she should do it. But I have to say," he scratched his jaw, "since you come across as being so modest that I wouldn't have expected you to announce just how well you shoot a gun."

"I suppose that is a bit startling. Hmm…I wonder why I said it that way." Her fingertips danced on the grass in thought. "I must be comfortable around you, and I was just being honest. It's an objective fact, seeing how many competitions I've won."

Chris stifled a laugh. From any other person's mouth, that might sound like bragging, but he knew she was just being open and transparent. And he loved it.

"How many have you won exactly?"

She wiggled her brows at him, "Too many to count."

He didn't even bother to tamp down the laugh bubbling out of him. She was more refreshing than the pond would be if he dipped himself in it. And those gunmetal eyes were a very apt description for her, now that he knew she was a sharpshooter.

"What about you?" She turned to face him, drawing her legs out of the water and tucking them under her skirts. He wanted to pull her body down on his, just to feel her strength, gentleness, and authenticity.

Yes, he wanted to kiss her, but this pull he felt toward her was not exclusively sexual. He simply wanted to be close to her.

"I know you want adventure." She wrinkled her nose slightly as the tall grasses swayed behind her. "Where do you want to travel to first?"

His cheeks lifted in a wide smile. "There are so many places to see. Things I want to experience. I would love to visit the Leaning Tower of Pisa in Italy. The pyramids in Egypt. And so much more. I could spend my whole life traveling and not see everything I want to see."

It was his dream and sharing those plans with her almost seemed to expand the dream. It was almost as though he had been given permission to dream as big as he could. His heart felt light, as if it were impossible for any storm to catch up to him and lay siege upon him.

This was a moment made for dreaming and believing. He wanted to stay here forever. He laid back on the grass, soaking up her presence. They barely knew each other, yet they were so comfortable together. He scanned her profile, appreciating that she had many secrets for him to discover. But one night could only expose so many, so he let his eyes drift to the midnight sky. Stars were twinkling above. So far away, yet promising magic and light.

CHAPTER SEVEN

Six Years Ago

KNOWING THIS NIGHT wouldn't last, Chris tried to absorb every last moment. The tall swaying grass, the stillness of the pond, her calm spirit inviting him in. The beauty of her soul reflected in her face. He imagined her with her sisters, listening attentively to their gossip and their dreams. He could see her offering encouraging words if one were to come to her asking for advice on how best to prepare for a husband. He could see her reassuring smile and soft touch, just enough to bestow much needed strength and replenish their self-confidence.

There was no rational explanation for it, but he could even hear her talking her youngest sister out of mischief. Perhaps Mimi had wanted to exact revenge on unrequited love, or see how fast a pig could run. Regardless of the circumstance, he envisioned Nobi as the soft-spoken, level-headed sister. Similar to him. Perhaps he had finally come to understand what kindred spirits were.

Really, there was no other way to say it though, she was an angel. Ah, look at him waxing poetic. It was not his default way of behaving, but around her, something was drawn out of him.

He couldn't get enough of her. And somehow he knew if he was the lucky recipient of it all, he might not even be able to manage it all at once. It was almost as though she needed to drip into him, one drop at a time, so that he could fully appreciate every single last drop.

Like a good tea, this needed to steep.

So he let himself relax in the calmness and just take it all in.

When he looked over the inky sky, he scoured the stars for any constellations he knew.

"Have you found any yet?" she asked as if reading his mind.

"Not yet. You?"

"I'm still searching for Sagittarius. The Teapot asterism. It's my favorite. I love my afternoon tea."

How perfect. Of course she would be looking for that when he basically just analogized her to tea. Closing his eyes, he shook his head, unable to give that symbolism more thought.

When he opened his eyes again, in a flash, he caught sight of a shooting star.

He leaned into her, smelling her faint rosemary and mint scent, and pointed up with his arm, saying, "Nobi, look over there quickly and make a wish."

He studied her for a second until he knew she saw it because she closed her eyes tightly. He could almost hear her wish being whispered into the universe.

Looking back up to catch the star for himself, he closed his eyes and made his own wish. But he didn't use his wish upon himself. Her selflessness had imparted itself on him, and he felt compelled to give her something that she would never ask for.

He made his wish for her.

It had hardly been a conscious thought or decision to do so. It just felt natural and right. He only hoped he made the right wish for her.

When he sat back up and caught her gaze, she had a delighted smirk on her face. He wondered what such a precious soul would wish for. Apparently she was thinking the same thing.

"What did you wish—" Nobi's question was cut off by the sound of footsteps on the other side of the tall grasses. The two of them hunkered down a little further even though they weren't visible to the couple from such a distance. They themselves couldn't see the couple, they could only hear them.

A drunk laugh belted out into the sky. The falling star he

could almost have predicted with how ethereal the night felt around her. But this…impending drunken debauchery did not fit.

Thankfully, Nobi's first reaction was merriment. Her eyes went wide in amusement to what sounded like the two stumbling and falling down onto the grass several yards away. Clearly the couple was inebriated.

And if they had only been inebriated, it wouldn't have been cause for too much concern. However, as alcohol often did, the couple was also *motivated*, of the sexual variety.

Of course, Chris had that gut foresight given the time of night, the location, and the state of the couple, but Nobi was showing her innocence by not immediately recognizing the course of action that was imminent.

What was at first an amused look on Nobi's face quickly turned to one that looked awfully like panic.

They were stuck. They couldn't make an escape because if the couple did spot them, it could turn to scandal. He didn't trust that their actions could be stealth enough to go unnoticed, especially since they couldn't bypass the couple to return to the ballroom.

So in the worst way possible, they were actually safest to stay exactly where they were, hidden by the tall grasses.

He couldn't think of a more awkward predicament. It had been one thing the other night to feign a tryst to deter the husband-hunter, but to be forced to be present for another couple's…coupling…was beyond the pale. If he could pick her up and sweep her away from this, he would. But it wasn't worth the risk of being caught alone together. In all honesty, the drunk couple probably wouldn't notice, considering not only how drunk they were but also how focused they were on each other. But if they did observe him and Nobi…he couldn't stomach thinking of those ramifications on her reputation.

The panic-now-terror on her face told him everything he needed to know. She was mortified. She was an innocent. And she wasn't ready to be exposed to the carnal actions of a man and a woman.

As loud moans ripped through the air, her hands flew up to her ears. The woman was giggling and the man was provoking her. She mewled her delight and it was clear that they weren't going to stop any time soon. They had a very intentional destination and they were going to arrive there, no matter what. Likely together, and from the sounds of it, likely loudly.

The torment was still evident on Nobi's face. Obviously she could still hear them despite covering her ears, and it was only going to get worse.

He had few options available to him. He could interrupt the couple, disclosing his presence and asking them to stop. But...really, they would probably just expect him to move on while they continued doing what they were doing where they were. Thus, he would be leaving Nobi alone to fend for herself. And yes, he wouldn't be there, so in some ways that probably made it less awkward for her...but leaving her alone didn't sit right with him. Not one bit.

The best option (as far as he could tell) entailed him drawing nearer to her. Which, yes, initially sounded like a terrible addition to an already awkward situation. But he had plans for this nearness.

He slid close to her, pulling her against his protective frame. Then he pressed his hands over her own, muffling the sounds. She buried her face into his chest, and all he could feel was her ragged breaths climbing up to his throat.

Her body was shivering against him, and he knew it wasn't from the cold. He was certain she wasn't crying, as he didn't feel anything wet against his chest, but he could feel the depths of her mortification to the point it was causing him pain on her behalf.

Being a man of the world, he had experience. Not as much as some other men, but he knew his way around the female body. So he could view this situation through the lens of amusement more than discomfiture. Yet the grip his stomach was in was something new to him.

He couldn't run his hands down her arms or in circles on her back to ease her tension, because the worst part of all of this was the sounds. The most he could do was swipe his thumbs back and forth over her fingers. He wanted to kiss the top of her head because she was a treasure, but it felt too intimate. Especially given their precise circumstances. So he leaned his cheek against the crown of her head, offering what little solace he could provide.

Gradually, her breathing regulated and the tension seeped out of her body. Their breaths found a rhythm together and stillness, at least between them, was restored.

He was so concentrated on her that he hardly heard the cries coming from the couple. But hardly was not nothing, so he had to admit to hearing the final yesses from each of them.

Hopefully they would be done recuperating and head back inside soon. No matter. He would hold Nobi as long as needed.

After a few heavy sighs and normal breaths, he could make out the sounds of them getting dressed. Their moans had turned to murmurs and light laughter. He overheard the female ask, "Shall we return inside, my dear husband?"

Chris heard a light swat, probably placed squarely on the woman's bottom, as the man replied, "I don't want to, but we should. Let's go, my love."

At least Chris could convey that tidbit of good news to Nobi. Her ears hadn't been completely scandalized.

Once he was sure the couple was gone, he lifted his hands from her ears. When she looked up at him with questioning eyes, he nodded and mouthed, *They're gone.*

With caution, she removed her own hands from her ears.

"I'm so embarrassed," she muttered. As if he needed the explanation.

"It's all right."

The look in her eyes was so tender, he wanted to brush his finger along her cheek. Pull her bottom lip down with his thumb. Run his fingers through her hair.

He did none of that. Just waited.

"I can't believe that just happened," she admitted quietly. And in that moment, vulnerability almost sounded as though it were spotted with curiosity.

"I should tell you something about what just happened."

She raised her hand in protest. "No, please don't."

He laughed as he covered her hand with his own and brought it down to his chest. "Trust me, I think you'll want to know this."

She nodded judiciously.

"They were married. I heard the woman refer to him as her husband."

"Oh." That one word found rest somewhere in the thick air between them as her lips locked in the o-form.

"Isn't that a good thing?"

Her eyes drifted up to him. "Yes…I think it is. No, I know it is. I just…well, I never would have thought a married couple would do that."

"True, it's often a more forbidden affair, but it doesn't have to be." In fact, it was refreshing (though awkward) to witness that love and passion could be so alive after marriage. Maybe one day he would have that. "Are you all right, Nobi?"

"I think so." She nodded, looked down at her lap, and then back up at him. "Thank you."

Those two words lodged their way into his heart, and he wasn't quite sure why. He might have to ponder that later.

For now, he lifted her to standing and they walked back to the party. As he watched her reenter the ballroom, he didn't realize he hadn't let go of her hand until he was forced to do so.

And he knew, without a shadow of doubt, that the next time they met in the gardens, it would be much more intentional.

CHAPTER EIGHT

Present Day

WHEN CHRIS WOKE up, it had to be at least a few hours later. His head was still in pain, his limbs were still tied, but somehow his dreams of memories rejuvenated him. But it wasn't for a few seconds that he realized his body was no longer jostling in a carriage. Though he was still sitting on some kind of cushion, the small space they were in was dark and static.

In other words, there was no movement.

"'Bout time you woke up. We thought you were going to sleep all day," Lester complained.

Jax bumped Chris's shoulder as he moved past him to sit down. "We need some information. And we need it now."

Chris was pretty sure he didn't want to give them anything that they wanted, but he also had an inkling that it might be his only chance to get out of this mess. Earlier, he had overheard Lester warning Jax not to kill him. So...that was probably a good thing. They needed him alive for now. And he needed to be alive for now. As well as into the foreseeable future.

So...despite his chagrin at wanting to play nice with these two ruffians, he was probably going to have to give them whatever they asked for.

"We want the pistols," Jax demanded.

Except that.

Damn it. Why did these two buffoons want Sam's pistols? That had to be what they were talking about. Just before the house party, Sam had entrusted Chris with a package—two dueling pistols that belonged to Sam's father.

As far as everyone knew, those pistols mostly held sentimental value. And calling them "sentimental" was questionable. Sam's father had been somewhat of a dueling connoisseur…and well, it was not so honorable to be a connoisseur at shooting people. Even if he always deloped. Really, after the fifth duel, it seemed the man just did it for sport. But no, every quarter of a year or so, the man would become a riled up jealous lover (over nothing) and call a man out.

He should have learned how to call out an apology instead, but no, the man was reckless. Hence Sam's overcompensation to be an unaffected lover. As if that were a possibility.

But those damn pistols. Sam clung to them like gold. It was awe-inducing that they had been a bargaining chip for him against Wes. None of the Betting Buddies understood why Sam made that bet in the first place, but it was starting to become clear. Perhaps he knew their worth to a darker sort.

In Chris's mind, he still didn't see the full picture, but he was getting a premonition that it could soon be revealed to him if he was patient enough. True, they were worth a bit of money given their antique status. But surely they weren't worth abducting a duke over.

Jax kicked Chris in the shins. "Did you hear me, duke? We want the sodding pistols. Where the devil are they?"

Should he feign ignorance? Try his hand at a bluff? Or some other tactic. He wasn't sure, but why not start with the obvious to make sure they were all on the same page.

"What pistols?" he asked his captors.

Jax grabbed him by the collar and twisted the fabric. Hard. "Don't play the fool with me, *Duke*." The title crumbled off his lips like a moldy loaf of bread. "We know you have them."

"How do I know that you know anything?" Chris asked, hoping to confuse them enough to talk more.

"I don't know how you would know that I know anything," Lester stumbled through his words, "but we know you got them.

You can thank a footman or two for that." Lester guffawed as though he had shed light on the most startling secret. But of course, staff had to be involved. Chris knew that Sam wouldn't have leaked the information.

"So where are they?" Jax prompted.

"How should I know?"

"We know you got them because we have people on the inside. People who saw it with their own two eyes."

"Not four?"

Jax scrunched up his face and walloped Chris for his sarcastic reply.

"Shut up."

Raising his hand, using it in lieu of uttering a threat, he demanded, "Now tell us where they are."

Chris scratched his head not really sure why he was provoking these two. Maybe to see just how far they might go. Maybe to see what else they might reveal. But either way, he kept at it. "You want me to shut up or talk?"

"Talk," Jax grumbled.

"I'll direct you to them if we get back into the carriage." He was trying to take some semblance of control back in this chaos. This seemed to be the best way. Soon enough they would know that he was just leading them to his house, but maybe in that time he could think up a plan.

He could see a silent conversation being exchanged between Lester and Jax. And then Jax was grumbling as he hauled Chris to his feet. Lester must have been the one to put a hood over his face because he could see Jax's grip on his arm as two other hands secured the hood in place.

"Let's go."

Chris heard a door open, stumbled over his steps, but all the while was prodded along by Jax. A prickling sensation broke out on his neck, as though he were being watched. He shook it off since he couldn't very well look around with a hood over his eyes. When they stopped, assumedly in front of the carriage, Jax hoisted him up and set him on the squabs.

More grunting and complaining came from the two captors, and finally they were seated.

"How can I give directions if I can't see where we are?"

Grumble. Grumble. Jax's hand ripped off the hood, revealing the landscape just outside the carriage window.

Chris recognized the shack attached to a little pub he had frequented before, so he knew where he was. He tried to look through the window to see what caused that prickling sensation, but he saw nothing. For a moment he thought someone might have been on their way to rescue him, but if they hadn't acted yet, there was probably no one there.

"Go south until we hit the end of the road. Then wake me up for the next instruction." He wanted to trade each piece of instruction for information, but he didn't think the two would be willing to go for that. So instead, he planted a seed in their mind in hopes of reaping a harvest.

"I don't know what you want with a couple of old, broken pistols, but I'll take you to them. They don't mean anything to me." With that, Chris rested his head back on the seat and willed himself to stay awake while appearing to be asleep.

After a few minutes, Lester started talking. Chris could have placed a bet that he would be the first to break down.

"Old and broken? That doesn't sound like the right pistols."

"Sh!" Jax growled. "He's right here."

"He's sleeping, just look at him."

Chris hoped his slumped posture was doing the trick, but he really needed to commit. He let his body fall toward Jax, and just as his head was about to land on the burly man's shoulder, he was pushed back toward the door. He did his best not to recorrect his position.

"See? He's sleeping, you big oaf."

"Fine." Chris felt Jax's thick finger poke his arm for good measure. "Don't worry about if it sounds like the right pistols. We know they're the right ones. Our man saw them. Don't you remember?"

"Hardly."

Jax grounded out his next word. "He damn well saw them. And now we're going to get them back, and we'll get that reward."

"You think this is worth five thousand pounds?"

"It's worth it."

"Even though we're condemning one of our own?" Lester's voice carried a wave of concern as Chris tried to keep himself lifeless.

"Aye. Well, maybe Big Tall Tom should have thought twice before doing what he did at that duel. Two men dead. One a duke. He deserves what's coming to him."

"They've been looking for these pistols for a while. I can't believe our luck. What are the chances that we put a spy in with the right duke?"

"You know there's luck and there's stupidity. And we just got stupid lucky." Jax's laughter rattled through Chris's head as he tried to make sense of what they were saying.

Chris racked his brain for stories involving a man named Big Tall Tom. He vaguely recalled the confusion over Sam's father's last duel. Instead of deloping, he had apparently shot the man and killed him. It was the same duel where Sam's father passed away. There were suspicions, especially since no man had brought seconds, witnesses, or a physician. But they were both found dead with no leads. No reason to think other than that the dueling duke finally found his death match.

Chris recalled Sam being relentless to find and keep those pistols. At the time, Chris thought it had been a grieving son's way of remembering his father.

But now...were those pistols used against Sam's father's wishes? There was a crime here beyond the duel. And did Sam know about it? No. He couldn't. If Sam had known, he would have told Chris. Or at least one of The Betting Buddies. But none of the four knew anything. Chris had to trust that Sam was only getting rid of the pistols because of his cousin. Sam had known at the beginning of the season that his cousin Randolph was coming to town. And though he had been suspicious of him, everyone had cleared up the miscommunication with his last visit.

So was this all a great big coincidence?

Sam bet the pistols trying to keep them safe. He lost the bet but couldn't let the memories of his father go until push came to shove. When Sam had finally entrusted the pistols to Chris, it just so happened to be at the same time new staff (apparently spies) noticed the exchange.

And then the house party had happened, so no one could take action. And no one took action against Chris until he was alone.

That thought—of being alone—that was the darkest thought in his whole contemplation.

Normally he didn't mind being alone. He was an independent man. Introverted. Liked—really, needed—time to himself every day lest he turn on some unsuspecting bystander. But this thought of being alone…right now. And then alone again once this abduction was done, he was planning on traveling the world…alone. Whereas once that had excited him, thrilled him, called to him…now, he wasn't so keen on all the aloneness.

It didn't sit right. It didn't feel right. Not one bit.

CHAPTER NINE

Hours Earlier

THERE WAS NO other choice. As much as it physically pained her to admit it, Nobi had no other choice. She recognized the situation in an instant.

She had been standing at the front door just about to leave, still pondering how to find Chris, when Jacob had emerged from the forest and told her that he had just said his farewells to Chris.

And Nobi could feel the twisting roots crawling over one another, forming a giant knot in her stomach. She knew she had to go after him. Now. She had to tell him about what she had just heard. There was no point in bothering the new groom. He was far too distracted to think straight.

Jacob had already gone inside vowing to pass along her well wishes to Sally. Nobi stood in front of her carriage ready to transport her home. But she obviously couldn't do that yet.

If Chris had just left, he was maybe five minutes down the road, she could catch him on horseback.

And there, of course, was a horse saddled up. Right there. Apparently one of the other guests was ready to depart soon.

If ever there had been a moment when the divine, fate, Heaven, angels, something—anything—beyond the physical, was prompting her, this was it. This. Was. It. Nobi's heart thudded in her chest. She had never been as decisive about something in her life as this. And no, she wasn't going to steal the horse. She was going to borrow it. For maximum twenty minutes.

The plan was to ride out, catch up with Chris, and tell him

what she heard. Knowing him as well as she did, he would insist on returning with her, and then they would sort out what needed to be done. Together, they would fix this.

So…although this was exactly the type of adventure Nobi had never asked for, she knew it would be over shortly. Or, at least handled by someone other than her. And it was to potentially save someone's life.

She could no more stand there and do nothing than could she not take another breath.

It was now or never.

Digging into her pocket, past the intentional gap, she tucked her pistol into the thigh strap that both she and Joan used to carry (more so than to conceal) their weapons.

She called over to the waiting footman to tell the horse's owner her plans and that she would be back shortly.

Then, she mounted the horse and took off down the dirt road with one thing pressing upon her mind. She needed to find Chris.

Soon, she had the horse in a gallop and was turning onto the road. After several minutes she could see Chris's carriage in the distance. Her heart felt lighter, just knowing he was in sight. But when a second carriage came into view, the foreboding feeling that had been festering since eavesdropping on those two men returned in full force.

This was not good. Not good at all.

Instinctively, she pulled back on the reins. Something was wrong. Pulling off to the side of the road, cloaking herself in bushes, she tried to keep herself out of sight.

As she watched two men alight the second carriage, she could feel her heart slam against her chest. First they took care of the carriage driver, leaving him on the side of the road. Then, when she saw Chris being manhandled by the two and tossed into their carriage, her heart ripped in two.

They took off.

She had to follow them. Where were they taking him? If she left now, or tried to get help she might never know where he went. God, her heart's jagged edges were raw and aching.

When she figured she could follow without being seen, she rode up to Chris's carriage. She called out to the driver.

"Are you all right?"

He groaned while rubbing his head. Then grabbed his foot in pain. "I'm all right, milady. Go after him. Find out where they're taking him. I can't ride your horse on my own. My foot." He winced as he grabbed his foot again. "But I can drive this carriage back and send riders after you."

"I–I–can't—"

"You can do it. Ride after them. Ride like the wind. Just stay out of sight. When the riders catch up to you, they can handle it from there."

She shook her head. She was not the adventurer. This was a higher order. Something more fitting for Mimi. Or even Boudicca. They were the strong ones. The valiant ones. The warriors. She was the helper. This was not what she was supposed to be doing.

But it was Chris. She had to get to him. Her heart would fail her if she didn't follow him.

With a firm nod, she turned the horse to ride.

"Go!" He called out, as if knowing she needed that final encouragement.

And then she took off.

It was supposed to be twenty minutes. Maximum. But the ride was turning into hours. Once she caught up to the carriage, she maintained her distance. When they pulled up to a tavern and yanked Chris out of the carriage, hauling him into a small shack, she muffled her gasp and stifled her tears. She was no good to anyone if she was a sobbing mess.

And those riders, she kept looking back for them. Waiting. Why hadn't they caught up to her yet? Had they lost her trail? Had the driver not returned to the house?

Too many questions that would go unanswered for now threatened to overwhelm her. But she remained focused on her task. Follow Chris.

She had one mission. Know his whereabouts.

Just when a plan came to her that she could try to enlist the help of some men from the tavern to storm the shack, she saw the three men leaving it. Chris had a dark hood over his face, but she knew it was him. It looked as though he could walk, and he didn't seem beaten up. That much was a small relief.

Obviously the men wanted something from him, but for the life of her, she didn't know what that was. She wasn't even sure she wanted to know.

Once their carriage was on its way, she again followed them. As close as she dared.

As they continued, she found herself on a long straight stretch of road. It was dangerous now. It was highly unusual for a woman to be traveling on her own. On a horse. For all to see. Riding astride, with her skirts pulling in a slightly revealing way.

It was beyond awkward and unsettling. It was precarious. If they saw her…there was no chance in hell that they wouldn't recognize her if they saw her again. She could be caught. It wouldn't be the worst thing to be caught if she was with Chris, but really, if they were both bound up they were no help to each other. She had to keep her distance…

So long as they didn't see her.

At just that moment, a skinny head with floppy hair popped out of the carriage window. Of course he had to go and do that now. On this road. At this moment. Dash it all. Her cover might be blown. The head looked around and caught sight of her, locking in on her and the horse. She had been spotted, there was no doubt. She was the only other traveler on the road. It made sense that from time to time they would want to survey their surroundings. Clearly, they were up to something nefarious.

It was useless to think that the man wouldn't recognize her if she continued to shadow them. And it would be quite suspicious if she (on a horse) were to maintain her position behind them, since she was obviously the faster of the two modes of transportation. It was expected that she would pass them.

Perhaps she *should* ride by them.

A plan was formulating in her mind. This road led to Chris's main estates. If she were able to ride ahead of them, she might have a way to stay on their trail even though she would be in front of them.

If she rode on by them and found a place to pull over and watch if they turned down the road to Chris's castle, then she might be able to continue tracking them. The trees were her friends. She could duck behind a small cluster once far enough down the road, and then she would lay in wait.

Lay in wait? Who was she? She had no idea how to deal with the manifesting emotions within her. Namely, terror. Was this the type of adventure some people craved? She thought not. Not many people thrived on living this close to death.

Death?

Tears threatened to pour from her eyes. She couldn't think about that possibility right now. Chris, despite his dreams, had always been something stable in her life. He was always there. For her. For his friends. For people. For his father. He had sacrificed everything, putting his own dreams on hold, to take care of his father. He was a truly selfless man, and now he might die? Having never lived his dreams?

No.

Hell, no.

She would do everything in her power to ensure he lived and one day could follow his dreams. If anyone deserved it, he did.

Her heart, though hammering, was flooding. How did a hammer feel moving in water? Now she knew, as that was the sensation within her.

No matter what happened, she had to follow Chris. And passing the carriage, lying in wait, and attempting to get one step ahead of the abductors were her next tasks.

That was the plan anyway, no matter how terrifying and assuming it was.

But it was her best chance.

With all the dignity and guilelessness that she could muster, Nobi trotted past the carriage. As she did so, she sent up multiple prayers for her own safety and that of Chris. She was sure the curtains in the windows shook as she went by. So she added another prayer. That somehow, some way they wouldn't take the time to memorize her face.

Her legs were shaking under her skirts as she approached the carriage. Sweat dripped down her back, and with clammy hands, she gripped the reins more tightly. Quietly she clucked her tongue to the horse to pass the carriage. Thankfully the horse paid no mind to his surroundings other than to continue on the straight and narrow. If there was a way to still her erratic heart, or untangle the knots in her stomach, or loosen the lump in her throat, she would have paid good money to do so. But as it were, there was no diminishing the tight coiling of her body. She could only manage to keep as pleasant a look as was possible (given her state) plastered to her face.

She didn't bother with a glance at the window. If, perchance, she did see Chris through the glass, she wasn't sure she could keep the recognition (or other emotions) off of her face.

Once she passed them, she kept trotting ahead until she was far enough away that there was finally a slight curve in the road. Trees lined the road, as if divining the perfect hiding spot. Gently, she tugged the reins and led the horse into hiding.

Now she had to wait. Wait and watch. Watch and wait. Time could not tick by more slowly than when a woman was waiting for a man to show up for her. But waiting was all she could do. Birds chirped in the trees above without a care in the world. How no one else knew of what was threatening to decimate her world, she didn't understand. It was one of the universe's tricks. That one person's entire world could be crumbling, but no one else knew. No one else felt it. Yet she felt nothing but this moment.

It was enough to entice her to rest and regroup. But she dared not leave her sentry. The birds could chirp, the trees could sway without worry. She would carry the burden no matter how heavy it got, no matter how far it took her.

The horse nickered, and the puff of air disrupted her thoughts. She only wished she had water and food for her horse. At least he was plucking away at some grass while they bided their time. Another seemingly unaffected entity in the universe. And that was a strange thought. This horse was helping her with what had to be the most dangerous activities she had ever endeavored to take before, and he was equanimity personified. Animal-ified?

Maybe this horse, the birds chirping, the tree branches swaying were exactly what she needed in this moment. With her world being ripped apart at the seams, or a better analogy, shot at as if it were target practice, she was due for something to balance the scales. With the deepest inhalation she had taken all day, Nobi took a moment to gird herself. To breathe in the calmness and allow it to permeate the tension within her body. She needed every ounce of peace she could collect.

It was certainly an awkward place to be though. Waiting for something bad yet willing something good to happen.

Never had she felt so awkward in all of her life. Well…actually, that wasn't true. Not that she really wanted to recall it here and now…but there was at least that one another time.

CHAPTER TEN

Six Years Ago

Last night Nobi had the most emotionally riveting and draining experience of her life. So standing here, at another ball, she almost felt too raw to be in attendance. But she remained vigilant because she had an important task to complete tonight.

Not like last night's incident. The awkwardness she felt almost surpassed the height of any other emotion she had ever felt…except…except that she had been wrapped in Chris's arms. With his hands over hers. Those soft, warm hands insulating her from something she wasn't ready to know. His chest offering her a hiding place. His body a physical protection for her. And that emotion, of being in his arms…that feeling of being shielded…guarded…treasured…

That was the apex of any emotional experience she had ever had.

She cherished the memory. Some men might have laughed at her naivety. Some might have teased her. Some might have coaxed her into learning, saying she couldn't hide under a rock forever. And she didn't want to live in her shelter forever…that was true. But she enjoyed her safety. Her comfort.

Though she wanted to know about the actions of a man with a woman, she hadn't been ready last night. She didn't want it sprung on her. It terrified her to be put in that situation. So the fact that Chris was the ultimate gentleman, showing her respect and compassion, had melted her heart toward him even more.

There was something growing between them, even in only

their two short encounters. They had an unspoken instinct to protect each other. Was it that they were both very conscientious people and would have acted that way with anyone? It was impossible to say...yet, Nobi didn't think that was the full explanation.

There was a chemistry that came to life when she was around him. And though she didn't want to admit that, because clearly he wasn't the man she was going to marry, in all good conscious, she couldn't deny it. He wanted adventure. She wanted to settle. Their goals in life were in direct conflict. And when she stopped to think about it, which she did a fair bit, she wanted him to live his dreams. She would never be the type of wife to hold her husband back from pursuing everything he wanted out of life. That's why it was so important that they want the same things in life. If they both had the same desires, the same vision, it would be the easiest thing in the world to support him, encourage him, push him.

But the ultimate sigh was still wedged in her chest. Other than his entire outlook on life...he was perfect.

So perhaps...perhaps that made him perfect for something else.

And just perhaps...that made her ready for the something she hadn't been ready for before.

So far, the two encounters with Chris had been by chance. Though really, the second one she couldn't help but look around for him while she waited at the pond. She would be a liar if she said she didn't hope to see him.

But if she wanted a third encounter—which she did—then she wanted to make sure it happened with absolute certainty.

And there were at least two very important reasons for that. One, she wanted to see him again. Just be around him. Talk to him. Two, she didn't want to be awkward about...sexual...acts anymore.

Chris was a safe place. Perhaps one of the safest she could have devised. He was respectful. Honest. And most significantly, protective. If she asked him for a favor, he would say yes, and he would do everything in his power to protect her. She knew that instinctively. No, there was a greater depth of knowledge than instinct. It was a soul-knowing.

And despite the blood pumping massive loads through her veins, she was here to ask him a favor. A very specific favor.

So she needed to be here at this ball tonight, find him, and sneak out again together.

Her eyes darted around the room, catching sight of the candlelight flickering on faces and shimmering against the gowns. None of that mattered except to find one face.

There he was. In the company of three friends, he sipped a drink. He must have felt her eyes on him because he looked up at her over the rim of his glass.

A half smirk lifted his lips as his gaze seared itself into her brain.

Those eyes. Serene blue eyes. The kind of seaside blue that invited a person in for a swim. Mmm…better, the warm blue of a bath that promised comfort and relaxation.

Only, she probably couldn't see that blue from her vantage point. But she could still picture it as if he were standing right in front of her.

And then he was right in front of her. Rather, just to the side of her, pretending to grab another drink even though his current glass was still half full. He wouldn't just walk up to her in a ballroom, having not been properly introduced to her yet.

This was her chance.

"I want to see you again," she breathed softly. When he didn't move, she wasn't sure if he heard her. She tried again behind her fan. "C-can I see you again? Tonight? In the garden?"

"There's a fountain by the rose garden. Fifteen minutes." His raspy voice tickled over her skin as she nodded.

When he turned to leave, she wasn't sure if she imagined the whole thing. His body language gave away nothing. Only the almost imperceptible nod he gave her when he turned back around was confirmation of the conversation she had just had. That of planning a tryst. Well...not exactly. Or at least...not that he knew of.

Fifteen minutes had never ticked by so slowly. She told her sisters the code word and tried not to run to the garden. It took all her willpower to place toe *and* heel on the ground as she discreetly slipped out of the room.

She easily found the rose garden by following the scent in the air. From there, she could see the fountain and a stone bench. There were hedges offering many places for a couple to conceal themselves.

Her heart was galloping wildly in her chest as she waited for him. Was she too eager? Yes. Did she care? No. But had she been reckless? Had anyone seen her? She could only hope that her senses hadn't entirely abandoned her.

She lowered herself to the stone bench, preparing herself to wait. But only a second passed before she heard a whisper calling her name, "Nobi?"

Angling herself on the bench, she turned to look to the sound. Chris emerged from behind one of the hedges, and she couldn't stop the grin from splitting her cheeks. Her heart fluttered like a butterfly emerging from a cocoon.

She watched him step toward her. Thick thighs threatened to bust the seams of his breeches. His broad shoulders cut the finest figure in his dark coat. She shouldn't be thinking these thoughts of him, but she didn't conjure them, they just floated to the forefront.

"I really wanted to see."

"I'm glad you did." He lifted his arm as if to touch her, but that must have been wistful thinking, because his hand continued upward to brush through his hair. "I was afraid our last encounter might have dissuaded you from your solo jaunts into the gardens."

"Yes, about that." She tugged on the fan hanging from her wrist to hide the slight shake in her arms. Maybe if she stood, she could disguise the waves of energy crashing down upon her. Rising to her feet, she looked up into his eyes, and she could see a slight furrow of concern wrought on his face. "I wanted to talk about it."

"Oh?"

"Well, you see...erm...that is," she dropped her chin to her chest, "you must know I'm a...well...you know, like most ladies before marriage...I'm a..." She couldn't bring herself to say it. She felt so foolish. If she couldn't even bring herself to say the word *virgin* to him, how on earth was she going to ask him for that favor?

A soft touch to her chin prompted her to look up at his face. "A virgin?" he supplied.

She could only nod.

"I suspected that based on your response to the situation."

"I'm sorry," she said, trying to pull her chin from his fingers. And she would have succeeded if his hand hadn't softly cupped her jaw instead.

"Why are you sorry?"

"I don't know." And that was true. She was flustered beyond belief with him this close to her. Touching her. For no purpose other than...what? She couldn't analyze the situation.

"Don't be sorry, Nobi." He held her gaze. "Don't apologize for being who you are."

"I think...you're right. I don't want to apologize for being myself." His steady regard bolstered her confidence. He was a safe place. She reminded herself. "That night was difficult for me."

"I understand."

"Well, perhaps you understand part of it, but I'd like to explain myself."

"Of course." He pulled his hand from her jaw, and she felt the loss all too keenly. He motioned to the stone bench. "Let's sit."

When they sat, his thigh was a solid wall against hers, and she could feel the heat through the layers. She wanted nothing more than to feel more of him. But she needed to go slow and steady.

"That night was difficult because it was uncomfortable for me to witness that," her voice dropped to a whisper, "for the first time."

Chancing a glance up at him, she only caught him nodding in understanding.

"And well, I wasn't ready for that experience. At least, not last night."

This time when she caught his visage, she saw his eyes widen slightly. When he didn't say anything, she continued on. It was best that he said nothing. This way she could explain everything without faltering. If he agreed to her favor, then all would be well. And if he refused, well, all would still be well. She just wouldn't rendezvous in dark gardens for a while.

"When I got home, I started thinking about it all. And I know it's expected that ladies should remain...pure, but then the wedding night will be such a surprise. Having no knowledge about any of...that, I feel at such a disadvantage. So..." with curious eyes, she looked up at him again, only to find his eyes fixated on her. A warm ribbon of a shiver rippled through her. "I was thinking that maybe you could do me a favor."

"A favor?" His voice was low and raspy.

"Just a small one."

"How small?" he cocked his eyebrow.

"Just a kiss."

There. She said it. It was out there, in the universe. In his capable hands. He could do what he wanted with it.

"*Just* a kiss?" he echoed her again while she nodded. "What kind of kiss?"

Oh. She hadn't expected that question. Um...there were different kinds of kisses? Dash it all. He was scrubbing his hand over his face. She must have crossed a line. What a fool she was.

"Forget I asked," she mumbled.

"Well, that's impossible," he muttered back.

"I'm sorry," she said as she stood up just wanting to get out of there now. She had clearly misread the bond between them. Or she had put too much hope into her request, not realizing how absurd it sounded. And now that she thought of it, it was asinine. What kind of lady asked a man to kiss her? She could shoot her own foot off.

His hand latched around her wrist, preventing her from leaving. "Don't apologize, Nobi. Just let me think for a second."

"That's fair."

"Sit down."

At his command, she plopped back down next to him.

When his silence continued to dot the air, she decided to speak up again. "You know, just the kind of kiss that you think a lady should have as her first kiss. On the lips." She had to qualify that. She certainly didn't want to waste asking her favor on a kiss like the one he had previously given her. Which had been incredible for her, but he had likely forgotten about it already. "That's all." She shrugged, hoping that might convey the cavalier nature of the request.

After a moment, he spoke, "All right." He turned to face her. "That I can do. Come here."

"Oh? Um…right now?"

He chuckled. "We could wait…if you want."

"Uh…no. All right. Now seems fine. Should I just…um…move somewhere? How should I sit?" She wiggled in her seat. "Or umm…what should I do?"

"You don't need to do anything, Nobi. Just close your eyes." When her eyes flew open wider, a small laugh trickled out from him again. "Well, that's the opposite of what I suggested, but if you'd like your eyes open, you can do that of course."

"Oh well, I don't…um…want to be strange about all of this."

"All of this is a little bit strange, but—uh uh uh, don't apologize—strange is sometimes just perfect."

She nodded and his hands found her jaw again. This time both hands framed her face.

"I'm going to kiss you now."

As if nodding was all her body was capable of, her silly head just bobbed up and down again in response to him. But actually, that wasn't all her body was capable of. In fact, her body was capable of a whole lot more than she ever expected. Namely, a fire burning inside of her and a tightness coiling between her legs. An ache. Already she was aching for more of him.

Gradually his face drew closer to her, and without her consent, her eyes did close. Initially she had thought she wanted to see every second of this first kiss, but somehow it was more important to feel it.

Just as she felt his breath against her chin, she blurted out with her eyes still closed, "What should I do with my hands?"

"You can do whatever you want."

"I don't know what I want to do."

With a rumble, Chris said, "Put them on my chest for now."

She couldn't even bring herself to open her eyes as she reached forward. It was as if she were braver in the dark, without her vision.

Her hands reached his thighs first, a soft pat confirmed that. Why she had started that low was beyond her current cognitive abilities. She thought she might have heard a soft grunt from him, but she was too focused on her hands to be sure. Then she slid them up his abdomen, all the way up to his chest. It was hard...all of him...but at least she had something to hold onto.

"Are you ready now?" he asked gently.

With a smile, she answered, "Yes." And she *was* finally ready. The moment was upon her. She could finally receive her first kiss.

She sensed him moving closer, his face stopped an inch or so from hers, and then a soft graze of his lips brushed against her.

It felt as though a bolt of lightning jolted through her body. Just as fast as it was hot, his lips were gone. And so were his hands from her face.

Her eyes slowly opened, and she dropped her hands into her lap. "Oh..."

"You sound disappointed."

"Well, no, of course not. That kiss was nice." She brushed her fingers over her lips. "More than nice. I'll remember it always. Thank you for showing me what happens between a man and a woman."

"Wait. You asked for a small kiss. A first kiss for a lady. That's what I gave you. A man should show you respect and cherish you."

"Yes, thank you. You are incredibly respectful." Something flashed in Chris's eyes. Something dark and fiery. Something she had not seen before. It almost looked like anger, but that couldn't be right. "At least, I'll be more prepared for my husband now."

"Nobi," he growled, "that wasn't a kiss to prepare you for a husband."

"It wasn't?"

"No," he ground out the single word as his hands gripped his hair.

"Well, could you show me a kiss…like that?"

His voice sounded strained. "You don't know what you're asking."

"You might be right, Chris, but I really want to know more. I trust you. You wouldn't hurt me. Could you please show me more?"

His eyes intensified and his voice took on a new kind of reverence. "I'll show you anything you want to know, Nobi." His hand brushed her cheek, sending tingles up her spine. "And at any time you can tell me to stop. You need to know that. If you ever ask a man to stop, he should respect you enough to do that."

"Thank you, Chris."

They sat for a second gazing into each other's eyes. There was a mutual understanding passing between them. A vow of some kind, but she couldn't put it into words.

And then his hand was back on her jaw, the other latched on to her hip. He waited for her to place her hands on his chest, and then he dipped his head and found her mouth. Open on a gasp.

CHAPTER ELEVEN

THE FIRST KISS had been chaste. And yes, without a doubt, it was a *nice* first kiss. Nothing too strong, impulsive, or wild. She had asked for a kiss that a lady should receive as her first kiss. And that was all well and good and all…a woman deserved respect. Deserved to be treated with honor and consideration. But also, a woman wanted to feel like…well, a woman.

All the gossip she had ever heard about women kissing and doing more (which, truthfully hadn't been all that much) led her to believe that there was something very forbidden, very tempting about a kiss—or more?—with a man. So when the first kiss came and went, and jolted her into a new state of being, she felt as though it was like a door opening. A door that she had never appreciated being there in the first place.

And now it was flung wide open. It was nice to see through the door and be exposed to the fact that there was another world out there, beyond what she knew. So, yes, that first kiss was nice.

But it was nothing like the kiss Nobi found herself in now. The door? What door? It had been blasted apart, with nothing remaining. Just a deep, wide open cavern leading to depths unknown.

Now, Chris's mouth was latched on to hers, pressing her lips. Tenderly. His hand was cinched at her hip, tighter than any corset had been tied around her. It was tight with need battling restraint. She could feel it emanating from him, and her body was thirstily absorbing it.

And the sounds. God, the sounds were different. The chaste kiss had been over and done with a small pop. But now...there was moaning. There was a rumble coming from Chris that was shaking her to her core while her own moans couldn't be squelched. It was their own language. Moan for groan. Groan for moan. And back again.

He angled his face to get more access to her mouth, slanting his lips against her. Her chest was weighted down, finding it hard to breathe, but breathing him in as much as she could. And her breasts were heavy. Waiting for something. She wanted to tell them to be patient and wait. Good things happened to those who waited, but she had no clue if it was true or not. No clue what they were waiting for, nor if it would happen or not.

But she was pretty sure she wanted Chris to do whatever he wanted to do with her. It was like her body was primed only for him.

And then his tongue swept out of his mouth and trailed her bottom lip.

On a small gasp, her eyes flew up and found his.

"Stop?" he asked, breathlessly.

"Please," she was panting for him, "don't stop."

And then both of his hands cinched around her hips and dragged her onto him, rolling her over his thighs and a bulge that found her center. Oh, that bulge. It was almost too much to think about right now. Her lips were tingling. The whole left side of her body was painted in goosebumps.

His tongue whirled through her mouth, then retreated to allow him to catch his breath.

And those goosebumps? They had all multiplied exponentially. Her entire body was covered in them. Her skin sensitive to the touch. Her mouth hungry for more of him.

"Chris," she sighed.

He pressed his forehead into hers. "I'll stop, Nobi. Just tell me."

"No, I don't want you to stop." She leaned in, pressing her aching nipples against his chest, finding short-lived relief. When her mouth found his ear, she whimpered, "Please, show me more."

With a growl, he took her mouth again, this time his tongue swept into her mouth and danced around. Devouring her. Feasting on her.

Her hands, that had been firmly placed on his chest, were now on his shoulders, and it wasn't enough. She needed more of him. More of his safety. His comfort. More of his demands. His growls. He was a dichotomy. Soft and hard. So hard. Everywhere. Gentle yet firm. He was respectful yet she could sense the desire bordering on greed for her.

Her hands migrated up the solid tower of his neck and with his groans as her guide, she lingeringly perused the back of his head and into his hair. Stroke for stroke, she tunneled her fingers into his soft hair while his hands crept up her ribcage.

And stroke for stroke, his tongue asked and answered the call into her mouth.

Tongues whirled. Hands explored. Her knees were clasped at his hips. If it was possible to be closer to him, she wanted it.

He was perfect. He called to her in a way that she didn't know could exist. Something from his depths beckoned her out of the darkness and into the light. Into his light. Into his arms. His protection. His passion.

A soft mewl escaped her lips as she thought of how much *man* she could have from him. It was as though her body never truly understood what it meant to be a woman until she was in his arms.

The pads of his thumbs grazed the bottom of her breasts. The sides. God, she needed more. When his hands trickled down her ribcage, she arched her breasts up to him and threw her head back.

"Please, Chris. More," she begged him.

His fingers raced up to her bodice, pushing her breasts up as far as they could go without bursting the seams. His tongue licked down her bosom and under the bodice.

"Yes," she cried out.

His breaths were shallow and his voice hoarse as he whispered to her, "I'm going to lick your breasts, Nobi. I'm going to suck on your nipples, and you're going to beg for more."

In disbelief, she echoed, "More?"

"Yes, more, my darling. Do you want more? Or should I stop now?"

She took his face in her hands and kissed him with everything she had. It was sloppy. She was too new to kissing to make it pretty, but she wanted him to know her desire was for him. That her desire had a heart of its own, and that her heart, despite her hesitations, was being firmly placed in his hands.

She licked into his mouth, tasting him. The faint flavors of tea and whiskey infused themselves on her tongue, and she couldn't get enough of him. When she pulled away, his heavy lidded eyes told her of his own desire.

Then she felt that bulge swelling between her legs. She rolled over it, and pleasure shot up her spine and down her shoulders.

She shuddered, "Uhhh." And before she could finish conveying her pleasure, his hand dipped into her bodice and pulled out one of her white golden orbs. His tongue found her nipple and she ground her core against his thickening cock.

His growl steadily sunk into her skin. He was respectful, but he had an untamed side. A beast. Something feral that was caged inside, clawing to get out. To get at her. And that's all she wanted. To be wanted. To be taken. To be treated like a woman.

The sensations of ecstasy swept through her while he sucked on her nipple. With a soft nip, she cried out, planting her hands on the side of his head. Not ready for him to move, but willing away that cautionary side of herself.

Him.

She wanted him. She wanted to know how to fix that ache inside of her, between her legs.

"Chris," she mumbled as she slowly moved her hips over him, "I don't know what I'm doing."

"You're perfect, Nobi. Just do what feels good. There's nothing you could do that would be wrong with me." His lips found her neck and kissed. A soft bite there and then he was back down to her breasts, lapping at the other side.

He let up for a second to look at her. His look was smoldering, so full of desire. "Take what you want, Nobi."

So she took his lips with hers and let him own her.

The mounting pressure between her legs was taking over. Never had she felt so wanton. Instinct was the dominating decision maker. It knew what it wanted.

She lifted up and rubbed herself down his cock. When he pulled away, taking a deep breath, she knew he was trying to maintain control.

"I want"—she panted—"to feel you. Chris. Please." Her hands fumbled at his falls, completely oblivious of how to take what she wanted.

He grunted, "Darling, there's nothing I'd love more, but we need something between us." He kissed her deeply, drinking from her lips. "We're not ready for a baby."

She didn't understand what he meant, but she trusted him.

"I'll keep my pantalettes on, Chris. I just need to touch you."

His hands reached down and undid some buttons, and as terrified as she was to see his cock, she was just as thrilled. Holding her skirts back, she watched him pull out his thick rod. Beads of moisture leaked out the head. As he gripped himself at the base, her body went up in flames. To her, this man was both fuel and flame. And despite the moisture pooling between her legs, she was pretty sure this flame was not about to be extinguished any time soon.

"Did you…did you just lick your lips?" Chris asked in a whisper.

"Did I?" she asked, looking up innocently.

"You're going to kill me, Nobi."

Without more of an explanation, he grabbed her and ground her on his shaft, rubbing her up and down his thickness.

With fewer layers, she could feel him settling between her folds, rubbing against her, tickling her, teasing. It still wasn't enough.

"Put it inside," she said.

"What?" Chris's voice was flooded with shock and desire.

"Put it in my pantalettes, so I can feel you more."

Inserting one finger down her drawstring, he made room for his cock to slip down. Now, just as his hands had once been her vice, her pantalettes held his manhood in place while she rubbed herself up and down him.

And, Oh God, the slickness. He was so hard, and she felt exactly where she needed him as she slid up and down his pole.

"Nobi," he said without almost no breath. "I'm going to come."

That meant nothing to her, they were mere words. But she could sense the yearning and the imminence of what he was saying. And she only knew she needed to keep rubbing herself against him. That pearl, that bud, in the center of her flower, needed attention. It was throbbing, Aching. Begging for something, and Chris was the answer.

And the pressure building inside of her was leading her up the mountain. Weaving through the trees, trodding down patches of grass, ambling over small bushes. It was like a path being pioneered, one step at a time. Each footprint landing on new earth, never before touched. This was unexplored territory. And although she knew that she was on an incline, she just couldn't see the top. Didn't know what it meant to rise that high. To be led there by the perfect person. Someone she trusted implicitly. More than could be explained. More than would make sense to anyone else. She knew him, and he was showing her a new way to live.

Just as the precipice came into view, she was hurtled over it. Falling in the air. But he was her safety net, right?

She called his name among some other words. He grunted, and then she felt a warm liquid pour out of him and settle in her pantalettes. When she rubbed him again to feel one last ripple of pleasure, his whole body trembled.

This.

This was everything.

So much more than a first kiss. How had she been so naive to ask for a first kiss? And to think it wouldn't lead to so much more. To think that she could kiss him and that would be it. As if that would be enough to satisfy something in her. It wasn't. It didn't. She only wanted more. And more again. This kiss and what it led to was everything. How it made her feel…she only wanted to feel it again.

He was her friend and he had given her exactly what she asked for. Yet he had gone beyond that, knowing what she needed. Knowing what made her soul sing and her heart dance and her body thrum.

This was…

Dash it all. She couldn't fall for him. He was meant to be her safe place. To show her passion and give her an experience. She trusted herself completely with him. She knew him as a protector. Someone who was loyal, caring, and compassionate. And when she asked for something, she could rely on him to deliver.

God, did he deliver. But could she remain unattached after this? Everything felt rather attached—sticky, even.

Every part of her was pressed into him. And she didn't want to unstick herself from him. Not even a little. Next time she wanted more. And there would definitely be a next time.

CHAPTER TWELVE

Six Years Ago

HE WAS STILL nestled in between her folds as she caught her breath. God, he felt slick and smooth. To separate from each other felt like she needed to release him, and she didn't want to do that. She delighted in the feeling of holding onto him in a way that she had never clutched onto a man before.

Never before had she felt so alive, so thrilled. So awakened. She had no concept of time. Had they been holding each other for ten seconds or ten minutes? It didn't matter. She wasn't letting go yet.

His forehead was pressed to hers, and as he rolled it slightly to the side, he kissed her cheek softly.

"How are you feeling, Nobi?" His hands rubbed her arms up and down, warming her from the night air, though that was wholly unnecessary. Her body was still on fire.

"I can't describe it, Chris." Her center could still feel his length, though it had softened, and the sensitivity between her legs was shooting stars up through her stomach. "I thought I just wanted a kiss."

He hummed his agreement, though she wasn't even sure what he was agreeing to since she didn't fully understand her own thoughts.

At first all she wanted was a kiss, but here with him now, with this intimacy, she wanted everything.

She knew there was more, he had told her that they had to hold back. *They weren't ready for a baby.* That was such a statement in and of itself. He hadn't said, *we can't have a baby.* Nor had he said, *I can never give you a baby.* He had said that they weren't ready. What did he mean? Uhhh…the pulsing between her legs was not going away. She couldn't imagine experiencing more with anyone other than him. It was utter insanity. Recklessness at its zenith. But she was a slave to passion. To Chris.

A soft mewl leaked out of her throat. She didn't want to leave. She already wanted—needed—more.

One of his hands was splayed on her back inching lower to tease her bottom. Through the layers of fabric, she could feel his pinky pressing into the top of her bum. And a shockwave rolled through her.

She looked up at him, glassy-eyed. Flooded with desire. Still. "Chris?" She nuzzled her nose into his neck.

"Yes, Nobi?

"I think I need more than just a kiss."

His lips touched her neck gently. A soft nip of her skin. "What do you need? I'll give you anything."

"Uhh…" she shuddered as she felt his cock twitch. She was so sensitive she swore she could feel his length hardening again.

"Teach me everything."

"I can't do that in one night," he hummed into her ear, tickling her to her soul.

"Start now. You can show me more another time. As many times as it takes."

His grip strengthened on her, pulling her closer, and without doubt, she could feel him thickening.

It was a heady feeling to have him respond to her so quickly. She rolled her head back and rubbed herself on him again.

"Nobi," he murmured, placing kisses along her chest. The cool breeze sent shivers through her nipples down to her toes. Pulling one nipple into his mouth again, she exhaled a shaky breath.

"Yes, Chris. There must be ways to do this without the risk of a baby, aren't there?"

"Yes. I can do that for you. For us. You want to do this, Nobi?" He drew his finger down along her collarbone. "You know what that means?"

She pushed up on her knees and arched her breasts into his face while she whispered into his ear. "I need you, Chris. All of you. And I think I'll need you again in the future." This wanton woman was unrecognizable, but she had to trust her gut. It was how she made decisions. How she took aim and let her shots fire. It was how she read her sisters and intervened only when necessary. And now it was happening with Chris. She didn't pretend to know the future, she just knew that this moment was important.

"This will be different, Nobi. If we start this, it will be much harder for me to stop. I will. If you ask me to, just say the word. But once we start this…it will take every last ounce of willpower I have to stop."

"I trust you."

His eyes darkened to an even closer shade of night as his fingers worked between them and he loosened her drawstring completely. There was no anchor for his cock, no resting place. But he was as hard as steel. With his hands on her waist, and his eyes on her face, he parted his thighs and slowly rounded his hips up into her.

And she could feel his head notched at her entrance.

"Is this what you want, Nobi?"

"Yes." She could hear it in her voice too, there was no disguising how desperate she sounded. If urgency had a name, she would have sent him a letter requesting more notice for his visit next time because he was pounding on her insides, begging for more. Begging to be let in.

Chris, on the other hand, or perhaps just on the surface, was demonstrating calmness and restraint. But she could see the toll it was taking on him.

She could ask him to stop. She could still remain a virgin, but she didn't want to. With a rare franticness, she wanted to share this experience with Chris.

Now.

And she wanted him to hear it from her. "Yes, yes, yes, Chris. I want you inside of me, please."

"Take me inside of you, Nobi," he murmured into her ear. "Let me fill you up."

His head pressed into her, she could feel herself stretching, sucking him inside of herself.

Chris's movements were slow, considerate, letting her acclimate to his size.

"God, Chris. You feel so big."

He shuddered at the words, an unbidden groan slipped out. "Take all of me, Nobi. That's it. You're such a good girl."

The pace was excruciatingly slow, but perfect, allowing her to soak up every second. Every sensation. Every breath.

When her pelvic bone met his, she felt him everywhere within her and enveloping her. Like they were in their own time and space. Nothing else existed beyond their connection. For now, in this moment, they were one. Truly together. She let herself sit on him, feeling him. As her hands trembled over his shoulders, he whispered sweet words to her telling her she was a good girl, that they would take this at her pace, that he could wait like this forever.

And her heart was overflowing. The moment was too big to drink in for too long. She might drown herself in the deluge.

Her body craved some movement, so she pressed closer to him, forward. The front hardened pebble rubbed against the base of his cock, and she cried out in bliss.

"That's a good girl. Find what you love and go after it."

She rocked back slowly, the movement singing through her. Forward and backward in erratic movements, feeling him inside of her.

She never would have dreamed that she would be experiencing this with him here and now. But sometimes life didn't provide the typical. Sometimes it offered the exceptional. She would be a fool to pass this by.

Looking for more movement, she pushed up on her knees, the feeling of her sliding up him, rippled through her. Keeping him inside, she slammed back down on him. A moan erupted out of her full of primal need. She had no control over herself, only a driving, pulsating passion for this man. For what he had to offer her. For how he made her feel whole. And wholly alive.

"Chris," she begged him for something, she didn't know what. But he knew. His hands were on her hips and his lips were latched onto a hidden part on her side. He was sucking and nipping at her. Slamming her down on his cock. Changing the tempo to keep her guessing.

When she whispered hoarsely, "Yes, there," he maintained his movements.

Her groans erupted into the night air, calling to his depths, again. Reaching for him. Offering herself.

"Yes!" she called out, her hands gripping his shoulders. "Yes," she whimpered again, this time her hands fastened in his hair. "Yes," she screamed, letting her arms go limp.

The wave crashed into her, over her. And then another pulled her under. "Uhhhh, Chris," she moaned his name as another ripple ribboned through her.

He thrust into her and growled her name. With a quick movement, he lifted her up, off of him, and she felt the warm liquid seep down her thigh.

Sitting her back down on his lap, he whispered something so quietly that she wasn't sure she heard correctly. She couldn't decipher the meaning, and she didn't care to. She thought he said, "I'm ruined."

— ෴ —

CHAPTER THIRTEEN

Present Day

NOBI WAS HUDDLED in the trees waiting as rain splattered down. Great. Rain. Just what she needed on top of everything else. Hopefully the pouring held off for a while. Though even if it did, her tracks were likely being washed away. Not that it mattered, she was sure the riders weren't coming. Something had happened to the driver, she was sure of it. She only hoped he was all right. If everything had gone according to his plan, the riders would have caught up to her by now. Surely. She wasn't that fast on a horse. Sure. Sure. Sure. Everything was sure and fine.

And even still, she was keeping pace with a fairly slow-moving carriage that had stopped for a period of time already.

How nice it would be if she could secure someone to help her…but she had a semblance of a plan at least.

Now she just needed to wait as long as it took to see which direction the carriage was going to go. If they took the road to the right, they were going to Chris's estate. If they headed to his estate, she wouldn't need to follow them so much. She could ride ahead—get ahead—of the ruffians. She could even try to set some kind of trap with the help of Chris's servants. What kind of trap, she had no idea. She wasn't like her sister, Mimi, always fabricating scenarios in her mind. Though…truth be told, those were a different kind of scenario. A kind of scenario that had no place in her mind right now while she waited for the carriage to turn right.

Oh right…about that.

If they didn't turn right, she wasn't sure what her plans were going to be. Just stay in the trees and try to be their unseen shadow. Follow them. Do her best to get Chris away from them at some point. Ride off together in the sunset. Well…no, not the sunset. Again…not a Mimi fantasy here. Chris was her friend. It would be more of a ride off together smiling, happy that he was safe kind of ride.

The only way either of those plans would come to fruition was if she didn't get caught. How did spies do it? The thrill of getting caught was much less thrilling and much more chilling in her mind. She was not the adventurer. Yet here she was. She could do this. She *had to* do this.

Just then, she looked down at her dress. Pale pink. Of course. That wasn't conspicuous at all.

As she was mulling over what to do about that bright fact, the carriage with Chris came rolling by. Thank God it turned down the road on the right.

She could trail alongside them in the trees, pass them at some point, and warn the servants. Lay a trap. If she could come up with a plan, Chris would be safe. Her friend would be free.

That's all that mattered. Her friend. They had made promises after all. But she pushed those memories away for now.

She had to think about Chris and saving him, though how she was going to accomplish that feat seemed utterly unattainable. She couldn't even pride herself on her sharpshooting skills in the moment. If push came to shove, she had no clue if she could live up to the task. Of late, her accuracy had been atrocious. There was no other word for it, and there was no denying it. Her mind hadn't been able to focus in the same way it had always been able to do in the past. That's why she had ventured out to do target practice earlier this morning. She might not have tried to squeeze in that small session before her trip home if her shot wasn't off.

So…maybe it had all happened—was all happening—for a reason. Maybe her shot needed to be off so she would insist on target practice for herself. That led her to overhearing the ruffians which in turn was the trigger for her to go after Chris in the first place. Perhaps it was meant to be. She would find him and save him. Somehow.

At least she had her pistol…she only hoped she wouldn't have to use it. Through her pocket, she rubbed her fingers along the embellishments, subconsciously yearning for its soothing effect. The memories it brought back were a balm.

After the carriage plodded out of sight, her hands ran down her dress again. It was a nice one, but, sadly it wouldn't be for long. She knew what she had to do. And even though she wasn't a proud member of the haut ton, by any stretch of the imagination, a cringe overtook her as she considered what she was about to do.

Dismounting, she patted the black horse. "Good thing you're already dark, hmm boy?" What would she do without the companionship of this horse? She was fortunate to have such a steadfast comrade for this mission.

And now it was time to get serious about her task. The horse was probably going to think she had lost her mind, but sometimes desperate times called for dirty measures.

So then, to her dismay, she plopped herself down in the mud (begrudgingly thanking the rain), and started to cover herself. It was…she had to admit…the first time she had ever done something like this. But if their carriage caught sight of her pale pink skirts through the trees, they would be onto her.

Was it overboard? Unnecessary? It might be. But she wasn't willing to take the chance. She was, however, grateful for her dark hair that didn't need a new coat of color. At least there was that…

It was taking too long to use her hands to cover her skirts, so she succumbed to the task and lay down in the mud. Cringing. Rolling. Finally, she sat up and started brushing off the excessive chunks.

This was all for Chris. Her friend. If she let herself think about the situation she felt as though she might just lay down in the mud and wait for someone else to step in. But she couldn't do that. No one was going to come. And even if they were, Chris was too…special…to her. There was something about their relationship that mattered too much to the universe. Too much to her. And she knew he felt the same way. They had made promises to each other, regardless of what happened in life. And those promises had resonated with her down to her bones.

This is what a good friend would do. They would do everything in their power to save their friend. She was his only hope.

But this hope felt like a millstone around her neck. What she wouldn't give to just be having tea with her sisters this afternoon.

The horse puffed out some air and let out a soft whinny. A shudder went through her. "I know, boy. But this will all be over soon enough. We'll get ourselves through this. I just know it."

When he stamped the ground, she was about to speak a few more words of encouragement, but a strange prickling sensation crawled up her spine. And it was not the good kind. Things couldn't get any worse than they already were, could they?

She was rolling around in the mud, with only a fast pistol and an unnamed horse as companions, on a mission to save her man friend from an abduction that she had no clue how to accomplish. What more did the universe need to throw at her? Wasn't she being tested enough? Wasn't this adventure enough?

But apparently things could get worse. Apparently she could be tested with an even more directly terrifying obstacle to overcome. Apparently, fate didn't dole things out fairly or in small quantities. This was her greatest challenge yet.

"Looks like you might be in a spot of trouble?" A deep, rumbling voice caught her attention. She looked up at a giant of a man. Sandy hair, light eyes, and a crooked smile. But was that a crooked friendly or crooked criminal smile?

Oh God, she could be in really big trouble right now. But not the kind of trouble the giant was referring to, the kind of trouble a giant could bring. She had no way of knowing whether she could trust him or not.

Sitting in the mud probably made him look taller than he was. Perspective was everything. But now was not the time for metaphysical grumblings, and now was certainly not the time to impulsively trust a stranger. Soaking wet and covered in mud gave her a new appreciation for anonymity. The man didn't know her. Couldn't really decipher too much about her either. She could be whoever she wanted to be. She could say whatever she wanted to say. She could do whatever she wanted to do. The freedom was unnerving. But not more so than his presence.

"I'm fine," she mustered with as much dignity as a woman caught rolling around the mud could manage.

He raised an eyebrow. "It doesn't quite look that way to the average passerby. Wouldn't you admit?"

"I'm not concerned with the average passerby." She waved her arm in the air, flinging a few droplets of mud in the still dripping rain. She wasn't sure if she was relieved or disappointed that no mud spots landed on him. At least it meant he wasn't too close to her. "Be on your way, sir."

"It's not in my nature to pass a damsel in distress."

Her voice firm, she retorted, "I'm not in distress."

When he took a step closer, her nerves tensed. This man could help or hurt her, but again, she wasn't willing to take any risks when it came to her friend's safety. She needed this man to leave and she needed to be on her way so she could get to Chris.

"I can help—"

She reached into her pocket through the hole that led to the garter around her thigh. Finding a good grip on her pistol, she brought it out, leveling it at him. Never in her life had she aimed a gun at a man before. Too anxious to take note of whether her arms were shaking or not, she schooled her features and said with all her authority, "I said, be on your way. Now."

His hands rose to the sides of his face in the universally recognized gesture of innocence. He was waving a white flag. And so he should. She was the one with the gun. God, she hadn't even considered what she would do if he had one. Inwardly, she shuddered at the thought. But she didn't let that show. She had to be strong. She had to dig deep. She had to be the warrior she knew Boudicca to be. She had to be the reassurance she knew Joan to be. She had to channel the intensity she knew Mimi to have.

She was a part of her sisters, always had been. When they forged their ridiculous duke dare, they had all been together. It didn't seem so silly now, that they had each committed to the dare, especially now that each one had snagged a duke. It had all been for her, Nobi. It would be her turn soon. Enough. Hopefully she could take the leap. If she wanted to do so after all of this was said and done. It might just be another risk she wasn't willing to take. She wasn't sure she had it in her.

Then again, her sisters hadn't done it alone. When Boudicca needed them to turn a blind eye, they did. When she needed them to help her make a hasty getaway, they were there. No questions. When Joan had needed a couple of pushes to see the truth about how she felt, the sisters showed up. When Mimi needed a listening ear and then words of encouragement, she counted on her sisters.

Whenever the three needed her, she was there for them. And right now, they were here with her. Holding her gun steady, she glared at him, waiting for him to relent and leave. Nothing was going to deter her from her mission.

With a huff, he dropped his hands and turned to go. His parting words were an almost petulant grumble, "I was just trying to be a friend."

"I don't need any more friends," she breathed out slowly. "Go."

He turned and mounted his horse, giving her a slow salute.

Self-doubt spiraled in her mind. He was probably a safe bet...but really, she just couldn't take the chance. There was *no chance* she was willing to take on Chris's safety.

Standing up, she watched him ride off. Then, almost unbidden, she muttered to herself, "I have enough friends." And that word, that precious word almost had a tinge of bitterness laced through it.

To most that word was treasured. It was a compliment. Sometimes it was a secret, but it was always appreciated. People bragged about having this word. People sought out this word. People strived to be this word. And up until recently (perhaps even right now), Nobi always cherished that one little word. It was something you wanted to have. In fact, most people wanted a lot more than one of them. But right now, she was only thinking of one in particular that she had, and the word just didn't quite do justice to Chris.

That one little word.

Friend.

CHAPTER FOURTEEN

FRIENDSHIP. THAT WAS the promise. But had it been the right one? It was a question she had asked herself from time to time, but hadn't been willing, or brave enough, to answer.

In this moment though, it was the question that threw Nobi back in time to a place she could openly admit that she loved. Bittersweetly, it was also admittedly a memory that played tricks with her mind. That time was about six years ago.

It had been two nights since she had experienced pure bliss with Chris. Two nights of useless chatter, meaningless meals, and forgettable events. Two nights of sitting at home, waiting for the next time she could see him. It was now the third night, and she was finally out at another ball. Wanting to look for him. But first...It had taken all her willpower to casually chat with a few guests (whom she honestly couldn't name now), sip some tepid lemonade (or was it ratafia?), and dance with (how many?) gentlemen.

She couldn't remember any of it never mind who she danced with, only that she had moved her feet to the correct steps (she thought), and now she could finally take a breath and do something for herself. She could search him out. Finally.

And thank God, it only took a second. Her eyes scanned the ballroom and in an instant they locked onto his. His penetrating gaze was dark, smoldering, and it sent a shiver up her spine. With that one look she knew what he was communicating. Meet in the garden. At the roses. Everyone had a rose garden, didn't they?

She wanted to run out there and rendezvous with him immediately. He canted his head and flicked his eyes to the door leading to the terrace. That was her sign (as though she needed one).

She told her sisters where she was going, entrusting them with her secret, and also confident that they would help her if need be. Then she slipped out of the ballroom and skipped over to the roses.

When she saw him, legs wide, firmly planted amongst the roses, she jumped up into him and threw her arms around him, knowing he would catch her. Her breasts were plastered to his chest, and her stomach plied to his. Pressing her nose into his neck, she inhaled his freshly showered scent. His soap was delectable, and already she wanted to taste him.

But before any of that could happen, she had to talk to him. Her heart had been racing for two days, and though she was sure they shared the same expectations, she wanted to be sure. He hadn't called on her, so she was fairly certain he wasn't reading more into their physical intimacy than she intended, but still…a girl could never be certain. Men had a tendency of changing their minds on the worst items. Now…if he changed his mind about being an adventurer, they would be having a completely different conversation. But men weren't wont to change who they were (only their minds), and Chris was an adventurer.

Besides, she didn't want to change him. She liked him exactly as he was.

"Two days is too long," he murmured into her hair.

See…exactly that. That was what she lov–liked so much about him. She was feeling the same thing that he was. But did that mean more to him than she thought?

"Far too long," she mumbled back. "Let's sit. We need to talk."

His body stiffened. "That doesn't sound good."

"It is good. It's just…something women need to do."

He chuckled, "Well, that is true enough." He took a seat on a stone bench and waited for her to join him before asking, "What do you want to talk about?"

"I just want to talk about us very quickly."

"Are you sure this talk is good?"

"Yes, of course."

With a trace of skepticism, he sat back and waited.

"I just wanted to make sure we stay friends."

The statement wasn't intended to be the harbinger of silence, but that's all that it produced. Well, that and a curious look from Chris.

Finally, he asked, "Friends?"

"Yes. I just…well, I've had boys as friends before, but well…it seems so foolish to say it now, but we never stay friends. So I invest all this time until one day they decide that friendship isn't good enough and then they move on. I want us to be friends first. Always friends."

"Friends?"

"Yes."

"Even though we've been intimate."

"Yes…"—she dropped her chin—"Do you think less of me for wanting to be your friend but also wanting to experience…the physical with you?"

His hand snaked around her waist and pulled her close. "No, I don't think less of you. I might even think more of you. You know what you want." He pressed a chaste kiss to her temple. "We'll be friends first. Always."

"You promise?"

"Yes, I promise to be your friend forever." She was too close to read the look on his face, but his tone held a strained note.

"Sorry. I'm asking too much, aren't I?"

"Not at all. Don't be sorry, Nobi. Here. This is how we'll know our promise is forever. I read about this way in Japan that a person can make a promise. They swear by entwining their pinky fingers." He reached his fingers out, extending his pinky while waiting for her to do the same. Then he wrapped his pinky around hers. "I promise I'll be your friend forever. And if either of us breaks this promise, that person shall have to swallow a thousand needles."

On a gasp, she almost ripped her pinky out of his grasp. "A thousand?"

"Would nine hundred and ninety nine be preferable?"

"Of course not...but..."

"Not so sure of our promise anymore?"

"Oh yes, I am. I was just shocked at the thought of swallowing a thousand needles. Or any number, really."

"Hmm...Terrifying, isn't it? Terrifying enough that we should both keep our promise, no?"

"Yes." She pulled his pinky closer to her body. "And we should also keep our commitment to you teaching me more about pleasure."

"You think the two can coexist?"

"Of course. Our friendship is strong. Though I have no idea how it grew so strong so quickly."

"Sometimes it happens..."

Nobi couldn't think of another time where she felt this way about someone so quickly, but she didn't bother bringing that up. She was much more curious about other things at the moment.

"Can you show me something tonight, Chris?"

"Yes, but in all fairness, I need to tell you about this bet my friends made first."

It was the only logical connection, but Nobi asked anyway, "Did they make a bet about us?"

He nodded sheepishly and dragged his hand through his hair. "What? How? Why?"

A soft laugh tripped off of his lips. "I'll tell you. But just to be clear, they bet about everything. I'm surprised we're all not without a feather to fly with. Perhaps it's because we're not losing so much money as it just keeps exchanging hands..."—he scratched his jaw—"could be...anyway. They bet about everything. So don't worry about it."

"I wasn't…" or was she? She needed to know the bet first to decide if she was anxious or not.

"I can see by your furrowed brow that it's best if I just tell you what they bet." He cleared his throat. "They found out about our friendship, and well…they think it's odd. They don't think men and women can be friends. Can you believe it?"

He scoffed.

She joined him.

"So in a roundabout twist, they bet me I wouldn't kiss you." His eyes peered up at her through dark lashes while his hand grabbed the back of his neck. "Little do they know…"

"You didn't tell them about that part?"

Shaking his head so a lock of hair landed on his forehead, he solemnly answered, "Friends don't kiss and tell."

His words, and maybe even more so, the tone, made her smile.

"So now what are you going to do?"

"I thought it was obvious." He smirked. "Of course, I'm going to kiss you."

"And what are you going to tell them about the bet?"

"I'm going to tell them that you're a lady *and* you're my friend." That was the part he spoke cavalierly. The latter part took on a greater depth. He peered into her eyes. "And just to reaffirm to you, whether we kiss or not, you'll always be my friend."

Her heart fluttered. In friendship, of course.

She took a moment to collect the thoughts that the fluttering had scattered. "So you'll lose the bet?"

"This bet means nothing to me. I don't mind losing it. You mean more to me than any bet."

More fluttering. This time with heat. She felt the gentle movements swish up her arms and down between her shoulder blades.

On a whisper, she said, "Thank you, Chris."

"Thank you, for being mine–my friend. Now...can I kiss you?"

Unaware of what he had corrected in his speech, she nodded as she climbed onto his lap, feeling safe and treasured. Feeling the depth of the promise. His intentions were clear and trustworthy. Her expectations were respected and honored.

Now...she wanted to feel a little bit wicked. She was aching to feel everything with him. The elation. The release. The satisfaction.

She bent forward and spoke softly into his ear. "Show me something new. Something different, Chris."

With a throaty reply, he answered her with a question of his own, "How different?"

"You decide. I trust you. Besides, I don't even know what I'm asking for."

"You can ask me for anything. If you know you like something, just ask me."

In a hushed tone, she agreed to his suggestion, "I will."

His hands cupped her jaw, and he took her lips in a hungry kiss. His lips were all over her mouth. Her cheek. Her jaw. Her ear. Down her throat. Licking her collarbone. Thinking she knew where he was going, she pushed her breasts up toward him to lick.

But instead of doing what she predicted, he nipped at her breast through the fabric, sending a jolt of pleasure from her throat down to her core.

With a growl, he said, "Turn around."

"What?"

"Turn around, Nobi. You want something different."

As she lifted herself off of him, she stood and slowly turned her back toward him. She wasn't sure how she felt about it until his hands slid up her skirts.

"Hmm. I'm looking for those pantalettes you had last time, but...my darling, did you leave those at home?"

And, oh, she knew how she felt now. Wanton. Wicked.

Yearning. For him. A shimmer of pleasure danced down her shins as she nodded. "I left them at home. For you."

The deep rumble of his groan told her how much he appreciated that little consideration she had made for him.

His hands slid all the way up her legs, brushing the backs of her knees, and in between her thighs. Then he was on his knees and his head was…

She was going to swoon.

His face was…

God, she needed something to hold onto…

His tongue was…

A shattering moan roared out of her. Pleasure crashed down on her. Her legs shook as his tongue swept between her folds. Feathering her nub.

"Oh God, Chris," she croaked his name.

"You're so wet for me, my treasure."

His name for her rolled through her mind like a boulder and settled down toward her heart. But she couldn't pay it much attention since his tongue was flickering against her nub.

And God, those sensations were overwhelming her. He was owning her. Controlling her desire. Peaking her desire. Edging her toward the precipice. She could feel herself cresting and then she tumbled over the edge while a flood poured out of her.

She didn't have time to collapse into a giant heap because Chris was up on his feet, then down on the bench pulling her backward onto his lap. Her skirts were up, and he was whispering in her ear. "Do you want more?"

"More?" she whimpered.

"Yes. I have so much more to give you. If you want to take it." He said it while arching his hips up and into her so there was no denying what he was offering.

"Mmm…" she moaned, grinding her bottom against his bulge. "Give it to me, Chris. I want it so bad."

She felt his fingers frantically unbuttoning his falls and then felt his moist tip slide up between her legs. Notched at her entrance, he asked. "You want this?"

"Yes!" she whisper-shouted. "Give it to me, now."

"Are you a greedy girl?"

"Just for you."

"That's what I want to hear."

And then he thrust up into her, their moans mingling and finding a rhythm of communication together.

His hands were lifting her up and slamming her down until she was biting down on her fist to stop herself from screaming.

This was what she wanted. To feel wanted. To feel so desperate. To be the object of his desire. To make him lose control. To be the one he wanted to lose control with. This was everything she needed.

White hot pleasure shot through her like a bullet, and it was chased by waves, pulsating waves, and then ripples of bliss. When he pulled out, she felt his liquid painting the backs of her legs. And when she sat down atop him, she felt him tremble against her.

This, she had to admit, was the perfect friendship.

— *oʘ)⊙⊙⊙⊙(⊙)⊙* —

CHAPTER FIFTEEN

Present Day

THIS RIDE WAS interminable. It hadn't been that long, he knew it, yet it felt as though forever and a half had already passed.

The scenery they passed, the rolling hills, the fields of heather, they were all blurring together. The clouds above coated the sky in gray, but finally the rains had stopped. The roads were muddy, but not too thick. The road was a safe one. Usually. He knew exactly where they were going, yet it felt as if they were headed somewhere new. This path that should lead him home was leading him somewhere beyond home. If he made it out alive and saw Nobi again, perhaps home would be redefined. And maybe that's why this journey tempted him to feel hopeful even though it was foreboding. Maybe one day he would travel this road with Nobi and they would comment on the delight of the purple coated fields. They would optimistically predict the turn of the weather. They would enjoy this trip. Maybe. One day.

But what if he didn't make it out of this alive? He smashed the thought in his mind. He couldn't think that way. He had so much life left to live. So much left to do and be. So many people he wanted to see. His friends. His family. Hell, he would take a kind neighbor right about now if that's the only option he was given. He had to tell Sam the truth about his father. He had to tell Nobi…more. Something.

And what of his dreams to travel the world? He had so much he wanted to still see, didn't he? He wanted to travel. The pyramids. The cathedrals. The food he wanted to try. The people and cultures he wanted to be introduced to. After all this time he had spent delaying his dreams (all for good reasons and without regret), how could he live with himself if he died before he got the chance to see it all? Well, that was circular thinking if there ever was any. He couldn't live with himself if he died before he had a chance to fully come alive.

And he wanted to fully be alive, the same way he had felt with...when...

Could he bring himself to admit it now? After all these years...

Despite himself, only one thing, specifically, one person was first and foremost in his mind.

Zenobia.

Yes, they were friends. But he had always wanted to be more than friends. He was just considerate of the line that she drew in the sand, the boundaries, the expectations, the respect she demanded. And deserved.

And he wanted to tell her. Even thinking about that confession caused more sweat to pour down his back than all the occurrences of the day so far...and really, that had been quite a lot.

If he told her how he really felt, he might be breaking the friendship promise, and a thousand needles was not an appealing consequence. Not that any consequences were ever appealing.

But still, if he told her, she might resent him forever.

The options swimming in front of him were blurring. He could die. He could die and never have told her. He could live and still never tell her. They would stay friends. He could live and tell her...and maybe...he could convince her to fall in love with him too.

It would be the biggest risk of his entire life.

The risk that would make or break him and his entire future. The question was whether or not he could live without her friendship. Hauntingly, the answer to that was a *no,* the likes of which reverberated across oceans.

So obviously that wasn't the question he wanted to answer right now. He wanted to ask and answer a new question. Could he live with himself if he didn't tell her how he felt?

Silence had never roared so loudly in his brain at the thought.

She was a beauty inside and out. Self-assured and selfless. A treasure that he had discovered by accident yet protected with the greatest of intentions. That first night in the garden, he knew she was his to protect. To care for. To love…But it had all happened so quickly, and of course a man didn't just blurt out, *I love you,* to a woman he had known for less than an evening. So when they had found each other again (and again and again), he let her take the lead. He followed her, yes he could admit it, like a lost puppy. But he took what he could, gave what he could, and he loved it as much as he could.

It felt to him that she was already his, even though the stakes had not been claimed that way. They knew each other better than anyone else, he was sure of it. And now life was showing him what it could be if he never took the chance to make that claim official.

He couldn't. He simply could not justify it to himself if he didn't take his shot.

He needed to come out of this alive. That's all there was to it.

A plan was forming in Chris's mind as the carriage neared his home. He wished his captors were only after the money. He could offer to pay them, then later have a Bow Street runner find them and charge them. Alas, they wanted the pistols as much as they were after the money. He didn't want to let Sam down, so it was his last resort to give them ruffians the dueling pistols.

He didn't think the two ruffians were violent, but he wasn't sure. So he didn't really want to risk any lives if he didn't have to. Which meant avoiding the front door at all costs. His staff was loyal to him. Most of them had been there generationally. If he could protect them, he would, though his hands were tied.

Literally.

Thank God that while the two had napped, he had been able

to free his legs. For now, and for appearances sake, he left the rope loose around his legs, but in a trice, he would be able to grab the rope and toss it aside. Knowing freedom was so close yet still so far away produced a nervous energy to trail up and down his legs. He had to work hard at not letting his knee bounce up and down reflecting those nerves.

As for the rest of his plan…that would take some finagling. If he could convince Lester, Jax, and their driver to go around the back way and stay out of sight of the servants, then he would be alone with them. It would be three against one, but he had an idea that just might work. His plan required a diversion, a tangle, and then making a run for it. If he could break free from the three, and maybe have only one to contend with, he might stand a chance. At that point, if he was running close enough to the stables, he could call for help. The servants there were at least tougher. Thicker skinned and stronger muscles. They would be able to help him. If they went through the front door, there was a chance the butler (well, maybe not the butler, but definitely one of the servants) would swoon.

Chris wanted adventure, but up until now he was the man who played it safe. He never took unnecessary risks, especially if other lives were at stake. That was James, though he might beg to differ. Chris wasn't even the type to get caught up in the competitions between the four of them. No, those roles were reserved for Wes and Sam. Those two would duke it out (in more ways than one) until the cows came home. If only they were here with him now…the best he could do was channel their wisdom and strength.

Jax was nodding off in the carriage, no longer stoically staring out the window. He was a big man, so Chris hoped that between the two of them, Jax wouldn't be the one to give him chase. The other one, Lester, was tapping his fingers, one by one, along the squabs. He looked to be counting something. Couldn't be the passing trees, could it?

The best way to convince his captors of his plans was to make them think the plan was their idea. So Chris started planting the seed. Since Lester had removed the gag a while back, he was able to speak.

"We're almost there." He tried to keep his voice casual.

"You would know," Lester replied curtly, still tapping his fingers. And yet, it appeared to be in sync with the passing trees.

"Yes. Though I don't know what's going to happen when we get there."

"Besides you giving us the pistols?" Lester cackled.

"Right. That. And then you'll just be on your way."

"Or something like that."

And that was the part, the *or something like that* part that niggled at Chris. He couldn't predict the future. What if he gave up the pistols and then they left him for dead anyway? No, he couldn't take that chance. There was only one chance he knew he had to take.

Resolved, Chris pushed Lester a bit more. "You're probably not going to tell me your plan, are you?"

"Nope," Lester said with a smug grin, the tapping ceased.

"But I guess you'll be trying to sneak me in so no one sees us."

Lester's eyes darted to his sleeping counterpart. "I can't be saying any of that."

"That's the only smart thing to do. I'm sure you already know about the back road that leads to the stables instead of the front door. It's the next right. Why am I telling you that? You already know that. You would have done your investigating beforehand."

"Of course," he scoffed haughtily. "There's no better access point."

"No. I agree. It's the quietest one. Unfortunately for me, no one will see us enter the grounds."

Lester leaned back into the squabs with a smile on his face. "And that's only part of the plan."

Within a minute, Lester had to "take a piss" so he stopped the carriage. Clearly he was giving new directions to the driver, but Chris feigned ignorance.

It didn't take long for the carriage to rumble along the back road, jarring Jax awake. "Where are we?" He grumbled.

Lester nudged him. "We're going the back way. Just like we said we would take if we found out that the pistols were at his house, remember?"

"I don't rem—"

In a role reversal, Lester slugged him in the shoulder. "Jax, you might have forgotten." He winked (sort of, it was more of an awkward blink) at his friend. "But this is what we planned. So no one sees us coming up to the front door."

With a low mumble, Jax grumbled a few more choice words and then rubbed his eyes to look out the window, more clearly resuming his position from earlier in the day.

"Let's just get there and get this over with," he added.

Chris was counting down the minutes, waiting for the expected dip in the road that would throw any unfamiliar travelers for a loop. He was counting on that hole still being there, especially with the recent rains, that hole should be nice and primed to give any carriage a good bounce. It was hard to see since it was just past the crest of a small hill, and it was highly unlikely anyone had filled it. The only people who traveled this road knew it so well that they just avoided it. The road was certainly wide enough to do so. Never had Chris been so thankful for letting something deteriorate before. It was coming soon, he just needed to wait.

It was tedious to wait, and it was overly optimistic, but it was his best chance.

No sooner had he finished that thought than his best chance was upon him. The first quick lurch of the carriage told him that the drivers had seen the hole far too late. The second lurch, followed promptly by a sway, confirmed to him that the carriage was going down. The final jolt promised him the diversion he was hoping for. The driver would be stuck seeing to the horses, and hopefully one of the other two would be distracted for just long enough…

Chris grabbed the loose rope around his feet and tossed it at the two men. Even if for a split second they had to untangle themselves, that would buy him some time.

Then he banged against the door, flinging it open, and he took off running. He had the distinct advantage this time, as he knew the lay of the land. If only he could get to the stables, or even within shouting distance.

Despite knowing he was still too far away, he bellowed, calling out to the stablehand. He had to take a shot. There was a chance someone was out taking a later afternoon stroll. There was a chance that someone was riding a horse in the woods. There was a chance…

But that chance was just not in his favor today. Because as he pushed forward in his agonizingly awkward race toward his house, he just realized that there was actually a much closer to *no* chance that anyone would hear him. He had forgotten that he had given them all the day off to attend the annual fair. If one or two remained at home, he might be lucky. But what were the chances of that happening? And that one of them would hear him. With his luck thinning, he still raced forward. There had to be a way out. And he wouldn't stop running until he found it.

The crazy thing about running and trying not to get caught though, was how many thoughts, how many memories, and how vividly they could all fly through his brain at once. In a single instance, a very significant portion of Chris's life flashed before his eyes.

CHAPTER SIXTEEN

Six Years Ago

"DO YOU KNOW what you're doing, Chris?" Sam poked him in the chest. The four Betting Buddies were playing a game of piquet at White's, and this was the third time Sam had asked Chris the question. It had nothing to do with the permanent grin that Chris was sporting.

White's was exceptionally busy on this particular evening. Men were playing whist, piquet, and a few new card games Chris wasn't interested in. Others were placing bets in The Betting Book on any and every inconsequential item of gossip floating around the *ton*, from who would marry first, who would marry last, who would capture the attention of the next diamond of the first water, and so on. Chris and his friends never placed bets there, only with each other.

There were a couple of men at the bar who were particularly boisterous. They seemed like good friends, though perhaps a ribbon of tension swirled through the air around them. Chris paid it no mind. There was always someone hankering for a fight, sometimes it was one of the four he was with, though usually not him. Tonight should be no different despite Sam's prodding.

As for Sam's question, Chris answered, "What I'm doing is, I'm playing a game." He threw down his cards to end the round. "Better than you I might add."

"Pfft, I doubt it." Sam puffed out his chest and slammed back the finger of whiskey left in his glass. "And you know I'm not talking about this game. I'm talking about a different game you're playing."

Not normally one to get riled up, the idea that he was playing a game with Zenobia caused his temperature to increase by several degrees. "It's not a game."

"What would you call it?"

CRASH!

All four men looked up as a brawl broke out near the bar. It was unclear what the two men were up in arms about, but before they could actually get up in arms about it, the four Betting Buddies were already on their feet making their way over to the two gentlemen. It was the two men Chris had noticed earlier and it seemed as though the tension had snapped in half and exploded. Now each man was rearing for a fight that was one punch away.

James whispered to Chris, "I bet it's about a woman."

"I'm not taking that bet. What else could it be about?"

James just laughed, but his laughter was overridden by a bellowing idiot. "I'll have your head for this."

"She already has," the man spit back with a sneer.

"Y-you!" The first man spluttered. "Name your—"

"Now hold on a second," Sam interjected, stepping between the two while Wes put a hand on the first man and Chris and James stood shoulder to shoulder with the second man.

"What's the commotion? You both understand the purpose of the club, don't you?"

Everyone thought it was a rhetorical question, except apparently the asker. "Well, don't you?"

"What's the point?" The first man, likely the more rational of the two, asked.

"We're all here to have a good time. Wouldn't you agree?"

The second man wiped his mouth in his sleeve. "Wouldn't you agree?" Sam asked a little more menacingly this time.

"Right."

"Aye."

They both mumbled at the same time. They were both still geared for a fight, but since it wasn't clear what the issue was, someone needed to dig a bit deeper into it. The right man for the job was standing at the center of it all. Sam could be both diplomatic and heavy-handed, depending on what the situation required.

"Right, then. What's the dispute?"

"He took my woman—"

"You mean the *harlot* we both see?" The second man jeered.

"She's no harlot. I love her."

Well, that was staggering. No one spoke for a minute. It was one thing for two men to frequent the same woman, it was another thing for one of them to fall in love with her. This was more serious than anyone had first expected. And it could surely come to that duel the first man wanted to instigate if something wasn't done, and quickly.

Then out of the blue came James. "You owe me fifty pounds," James whispered loudly in front of the second man's chest.

A little startled, Chris answered back. "I never took that bet, you idiot. And I'd never bet fifty pounds on that."

James scoffed. And then, when he said it louder, Chris realized his intentions. "You can't renege on a bet."

"I can if I didn't make the bet," Chris said with fake ire.

"You made the bet and you'll pay it off."

"We'll see about that."

And by now, the fake fight had escalated enough to diffuse the first fight.

"We'll drink for it," James baited him.

"Aye, we shall."

So all six men stood at the bar while James and Chris faked a round of shot-taking. The first to finish won, the other paid up.

Not even thinking about the purpose of the shots, all six men had soon joined in. Sam and Wes finished first, everyone else finished in the middle, and somehow, James and Chris each struggled to take last place.

"Another?" James asked with a big grin.

"Sometimes you have to cut your losses," Chris said, declining the shot.

With a dribble running down their chins, the two men who had initially been arguing were now patting each other on the backs, congratulating themselves on not having to pay the fifty pounds. Not that they would have had to in any case. In fact, not that anyone would have had to.

As the two former almost-fighters walked away with one arm slung over the other's shoulder, Chris overheard the concession. "You should have her. Ask her to marry you."

"I will."

And that settled that.

And it was a beautiful thing, seeing love shine through and win. Just beautiful. Albeit a bit of an awkward event that the four witnessed together. Chris had a feeling none of them would feel so kindly if one of them had slept with the love of their life, but he didn't dare say anything.

Then all was forgotten except the bogus competition. Of course.

"I'll take that money now," Wes and Sam both extended their hands to Chris, while he slapped them away muttering that he owed them. Quietly hoping they wouldn't make him pay up, he accepted that this was Wes and Sam…so likely he would be out fifty pounds. At least no duels had been called.

The four grabbed another drink and headed back to their seats.

"Don't think a little fight like that will deter me. I asked you a question before those buffoons nearly took off each other's heads. What would you call it? What's between you and Zenobia?" Sam asked.

"I've already told you, we're friends."

"Right. *Friends*," Wes chimed in using a mocking tone on the last word.

James chuckled. "I have to agree with these two bacon brains. Not sure you can be friends with a woman."

"We are."

"For now," Sam goaded.

Chris had to correct him. It wasn't just *for now*. And there was one perfect one he could use in his retort. That one word was on the tip of his tongue. And by the time he realized how it was going to sound to three very masculine dukes (some of whom didn't believe in marriage or love), it was too late, the word had slipped free and into the universe. "Forever."

Instead of the boisterous ridicule he expected, the three men sat stunned, staring at him. After a long beat of their awkward gazes trying to pry something out of him, he gave up.

"What?"

"You're going to be friends forever?" Well, when James put it that way, in that condescending tone of his, as though Chris were a schoolboy handing in an unfinished assignment…well, yes…it didn't sound that great. The idea of forever friends had certainly lost some of its flare; rather, some of its heat. But when Chris had made that promise to Nobi in the garden a few nights earlier, there had been nothing but heat, sparks, a veritable inferno between them. Especially when she crawled up and straddled his lap.

"Chris?"

The call shook him free of the vision that had been forming in his mind.

"What?"

"You really want us to believe that you're going to be"—Wes cleared his throat, as if there was some kind of barrier in there that was prohibiting him from voicing the next two-word phrase—"*forever friends* with Zenobia?"

Before Chris could nod his affirmation, Sam interrupted. "The better question is, do *you* really believe that you're going to be friends forever with Zenobia?"

Yes, Sam was insightful, deceivingly so. He played the alpha, but he might be the most intuitive of them all. After Chris, that was. That *was* the better question. Did he believe it himself?

"Laugh if you must, but we made a promise. Nobi is…special to me. We will always be friends."

"You better not hurt her," James warned, which surprised Chris.

"James, you don't even believe in love. What's the warning for?"

"Who said anything about love?" Wes piped up.

Sam shushed Wes, it would take too long to catch him up. Instead, Sam focused his attention between Chris and James. "You really think she'll be the first one to get hurt? Look at our boy already? He's off in some dreamland. Surely, he'll be the first to trip and fall, landing smack on his face. The man's dignity will be smashed to pieces."

Chris was not going to credit Sam by telling him that he had already fallen and that it was too late for his dignity.

"We're both adults. We'll be fine."

The game of piquet had paused at some point in their discussion. Now Chris was merely shuffling the cards to keep his hands preoccupied.

"You know she's a lady—"

"What are you implying, Sam?" Chris's voice came out evenly despite the spike in his blood pressure, and Sam's hands flew up into the air.

"I'm not implying anything. Just stating a fact."

Wes shook his head and slapped his palm down on Chris's shoulder. "Let's finish this game, so I can win and take my loot home."

"Ha!" Sam bellowed. And then in his over the top competitive nature, he clamped a palm on Chris's other shoulder. "You think you're going to win. That's endearing."

James and Chris exchanged a look of resignation, and in that same look, they both settled who they were placing bets on.

The series of movements eased any tension and the four settled back into the rhythm of their game.

After the third game was over, because ties were not allowed, and after Sam won one and Wes won one, they insisted on a tie breaker, which of course James won. So now they were onto their fourth game, Chris stood to leave.

James rose with him, stating the night had gotten away from him.

As Chris and James left the club, a dark-haired, crimson-lipped woman approached the two of them. Apparently she had eyes only for Chris, but he hardly noticed until James elbowed him when the woman was directly in front of him.

She was dressed for an evening of pleasure. Wickedness. The fragrance wafting off of her was pungent. And some man would be lucky to have her. Of that, he was sure. He was also sure that that man wasn't him.

In a sultry voice, she asked, "Ready for a night out with me?"

He wasn't one to just take women home. He didn't even know this woman, had never met her before, and her proposition was startling. It wasn't startling because of who she was, nor was it because of who he was…it was more shocking than anything because of where he was at in his heart. How his soul felt tangled up already. He was so far gone, he wasn't expecting someone to wiggle their way in.

Catching sight of her eyes, he saw the desire she felt. It was twofold. The first was for him, a man, to experience pleasure. The second was for more. He couldn't read the depths of it though.

And he didn't care to. He wasn't interested in any pleasure with her. In fact, he wasn't interested in any pleasure with any woman except Zenobia.

"No, thank you." He almost walked by without adding, "But I do hope you find what you're looking for."

As the woman walked off in nonchalance, James spoke up, "That was a…nice thing to say."

"Sometimes you have to say what you're feeling," Chris mused.

But James only joked back, "Not always."

"No. That's true." And that truth sent a painful sting through his chest. There were some things he just couldn't say right now. "But sometimes…sometimes you get to say what you're feeling."

On those vague words, James took off and Chris alighted his carriage to head home for the night.

He knew he had found what he was looking for already. He only wanted pleasure with Zenobia.

Yes, it might be a night or two before another ball. And yes, they may or may not always be able to sneak away and enjoy a tryst together. No, he didn't want to call it a tryst. It was so much more than that. It was sharing intimately together. That was the more. That was what he wanted. That was all he wanted.

And he would wait for her to have it. He would wait for as long as it took to have it with Zenobia. Only her.

CHAPTER SEVENTEEN

Six Years Ago

CHRIS DIDN'T HAVE to wait too long until he saw Nobi again. There was a pleasure fair happening on the weekend that he decided to attend in hopes of seeing her, and he was soon to be amply rewarded. He didn't spend any time trying the new foods he saw and smelled in the air. He didn't bother stopping in for a pint at one of the new stalls he had never seen before. And he wasn't even curious about the trinkets from the Romani tents. Yet.

Not without her at least.

Normally, he would have been lingering at each new place in search of curios or something to treat his palate, but they held no appeal for the moment. The only thing he wanted to do was find her first. Once he had her company, then they could experience the rest together; as much or as little as she wanted. He just yearned to be by her side. In a way, he was almost more curious to see her reaction to everything than for himself to see it all. So the search for her was all-important.

Of course he found her at the shooting gallery, where he had only been lurking—waiting—for roughly five—sixty—minutes.

When she approached the gallery, he sauntered up casually.

"I was hoping to see you here today."

"You were?" She glanced around the grounds, taking in the food and drink stalls, along with the various tents boasting of wrestlers, wax works, freakshows, a fortune teller and more. "How did you know where to find me?"

"I reasoned that at some point you would make your way over to the shooting gallery, given your impressive skill level."

"You've never seen me shoot."

"No. It was self-proclaimed."

"Oh," she demurred a little and then as if regaining her balance, added, "well, I suppose I probably would have said that. It is true, you know."

"I think I need to see it for myself now."

"You will."

Making the vow, she stepped up toward the fair worker who promptly offered the gun to Chris.

"Here you go, Your Grace."

With a gentle redirection, Chris said, "The first one should be offered to the lady, wouldn't you agree?"

A red blush crept into the fair worker's face. "Of-of course, Your Grace." He bowed awkwardly and then proffered the gun to Nobi.

"Thank you," she said, taking the gun.

Armed, the two took their stances in front of the targets.

"Where are your sisters?"

"They didn't want to shoot again."

"You've already been here?"

"Only all morning," she smiled at him. "I took the last hour off to do things they wanted to do. It only seemed fair." When his gaze swept over to the fair worker, she clarified that someone else had been working the earlier shift.

"Well, if you've been here all morning, you certainly have the advantage."

"Chris," she placed a hand on his forearm, "when it comes to shooting, I can almost guarantee you that I will always have the advantage."

A soft chuckle rushed out of his mouth. "Then let's shoot, Sharpshooter."

The targets were set up about twenty five paces away. Hitting the outer ring won the shooter a small sweetmeat. The middle ring won a toy solider while a bullseye was rewarded with a small wooden horse.

And if anyone was able to hit the tiny pebble sitting on top of the target, they would win the spinning globe.

"If you've been here all morning, what have you won?"

With a playful eye and an arched tone, she said, "I've been winning for myself. I pick a spot on the target not corresponding to a prize, and then I hit it. I did win a few sweetmeats though." She grinned as she patted her pocket.

"Right then. Shall we say best of three?"

"Is there another option?"

"Announce your shot and then take it."

She didn't answer, but when he glanced over, she was already lining herself up. "Wooden horse," she whispered. A beat hung in the air. The wind swept a few strands of her hair across her face, and she waited for the movement to still. Then the smallest movement from her finger triggered the gun and a bullet flew.

With a soft whistle, a small wooden horse was placed on the wooden ledge in front of her.

Chris raised his gun and called out the same mark. With a bang, another wooden horse was placed on the ledge.

"Excellent shot, Your Grace."

She had never referred to him that way before, and something about her submissive yet teasing tone caused a melting sensation to pour over his body.

He cleared his throat.

"You call the next one," she said.

"Globe."

It was ambitious, but he had to try. He took a steadying breath and then pulled the trigger. The pebble was much smaller than he expected, and he missed. He took his third shot and missed again.

When Nobi took her position, he saw the glint in her eye, as if she had been saving this shot for him to see.

Click. BANG! Plop.

The pebble slid off the target.

To say he was impressed was an understatement. Clearly the fair worker was equally impressed.

"Haven't seen that yet," he said in awe.

Nobi merely lifted one shoulder half an inch and pulled her lips back in a small smirk.

As the globe was placed in front of her, she spun it around, thinking of what to say.

"I'll carry it for you," Chris offered as he returned their weapons to the fair worker.

"Does it sound silly to say I won it for you?"

"No, but you won it. It belongs to you."

"You're the one who wants to travel the world. Not me. You should have it," she said on a whisper.

And though the words were said quietly, they were powerful. They forged their way into his heart.

He took a step closer to her, until he could smell her soft rosemary and mint fragrance. "For that reason, you should keep it. That way you'll always know where I am."

Her smile lit up her face like the sun appearing from behind the clouds. "Then I shall be selfish and keep it."

It took a few minutes to sort out, but Chris had one of his footmen take the prize and deliver it to her house.

With free hands, they were able to explore the fair.

Chris convinced Nobi that they needed to try as much food as they could. From meat pies to roasted nuts, and from toffee to a small bowl of pottage.

"I can't take another bite," Nobi protested.

"Just one more." Chris couldn't hide the excitement from his voice.

And a realization must have dawned on Nobi's face because her brows furrowed in curiosity as she said, "This is how you imagine traveling, isn't it?"

She understood him. Without him trying to show her or tell her anything. He was just himself, and she understood.

"Yes," he sighed contently. "I imagine traveling the world will have so many new experiences, like food, that I will have a hard time keeping in shape."

He felt her eyes scan his body and his blood heated up while his throat went dry.

"I think you'll be fine," she whispered.

"Then let's go try another one. How about the fruit stall? It looks as though they have some rare fruits."

"You try it, I'll come with you."

"It won't be the same."

She only laughed at his argument. "I'll try one more with you, but you must realize that there will be other fairs, Chris."

He placed her hand on his forearm to reroute them. "You're right. I don't need the fruit. Right now, at least. What should we see next then?"

With what he hoped was a twinkle in his eye, Chris said, "We should visit the fortuneteller."

Her questioning brow made him laugh, and he asked, "Don't you want to know your future."

"In some ways, I suppose...But I didn't think you would be the kind to want to know that."

"I'm not. But I thought you might like it. Besides, I've always been curious about the Romani culture. Let's go."

He wasn't really giving her a chance to refuse. Already, he had her hand tucked away on his arm, and he was about to drag her there when she blurted out.

"Oh! Let's visit that metalwork stall first. Then we can visit the fortuneteller."

They meandered through the light crowd until they stood in front of the table. It was a known skill that Romani were adept with metalworking. The tables were lined with exquisite examples of everything from bookends to jewelry. Chris watched as Nobi eyed a few pieces, but then saw her gaze snag on the far table. Immediately he knew why.

"I didn't realize Romani fashioned weapons?" he remarked to

the craftsman.

"We don't normally, but we have a few men who studied the craft."

Nobi's finger trailed one particular pistol with rose embellishments.

"She'll take that one," Chris said.

"No, I couldn't," she protested.

"Why not?"

"Well…" Chris read her body language. Her eyes and that one trailing finger were not in agreement with the feeble protestation emerging from her lips.

"Well, if she won't take it, I will." Chris stepped toward the pistol.

"Oh, but really, it's not made for…um…you."

With a wry look, Chris asked, "It's not?"

"No." She picked up the pistol and handed it to the craftsmen for wrapping. "I'll take it."

Chris piped up, asking the craftsmen, "How do you say *thank you* in Romani?"

"There are different languages among the various Romani groups. But we say *te danke*."

"Te danke," Chris echoed the words and the man nodded his approval.

Once the pistol was purchased with ammunition and wrapped up, they left the stall.

"I know what you did back there," she said softly.

"I didn't think I was being subtle."

Her smile was worth it. "Well, thank you. Te danke. Shall we go see about that fortuneteller now?"

"This way, Lady Zenobia," he gestured with a chivalrous bow.

The tent they approached was made of red velvet and had gold tassels hanging from it. Once they entered Madame Araminta's tent, they were greeted by a woman sitting in shadows cast by a few sparse candles. Nearly cloaked in darkness, it was difficult to make out her features. Even a scarf covered her head, only revealing a few strands which appeared to be the color of fire.

"Sit. Sit." She gestured to the chairs. "What brings you to Madame Araminta?"

"Curiosity," Chris answered at the same time that Nobi pointed a thumb at him.

A smile tugged on the corner of Madame Araminta's mouth, but she said nothing. After a beat, she yanked the cover off of her crystal ball and swirled her hands over the top of it.

"I see…love—"

"Oh, we're not in love," Nobi interjected innocently, or at least he assumed she was just trying to be honest. But the words sliced through him all the same. "We're friends." The two words were added with what looked like a hopeful grin.

"Yes. We're friends," Chris relayed to the fortuneteller. Though he thought a fortuneteller should be able to pick up on that.

"Don't interrupt me," she finally snapped. "I see greatness for you."

"Which one of us?" Nobi asked.

"Both of you. Now don't interrupt me again." Her eyes trained on the ball, seeing (or not seeing) something, Chris waited for her next words.

"I have not seen the likes of this in a long time. This is rare indeed." She exhaled a rough breath. "You will be forced to choose, many times in life. Safety and comfort or uncertainty and adventure. It is up to you. You must choose. The two camps seem incompatible. It's true. They are impossible to unite—no, next to impossible to unite. It will take—"

"Fire," Chris called out.

"Yes, fire, and—"

Chris was up on his feet now and hauling Nobi with him to protect her. "No. There's a fire climbing up your table. One of the candles must have fallen. Do you have some water?"

Madame Araminta was nonplussed by the fire and far too engrossed in the crystal ball, yet she waved her hand behind her head, muttering something about a shelf.

Chris found the vase with flowers in it and doused the small flames. The fortuneteller's words were ringing in his head. He had heard enough. Whether she read the ball, their clothing, or their body language, she was right. They were two people who wanted entirely different futures. Maybe he had been fooling himself. Maybe he had allowed himself to hope too much, to feel too much. To think the impossible.

She was his perfect person except for where and how she wanted to live. He wanted to argue with himself that those were insignificant in the grand scheme of life…but really, they were in some ways the most significant. They affected a person's initial decisions in setting up a home or a family. And if they disagreed and one person compromised, then every day, resentment would build.

They knew each other so well, and it felt right just being with her…yet, there was no denying—and apparently no uniting—their contrasting worldviews.

Not for the first or last time, Chris thought to himself that he would just take what was available to him. He wouldn't push her for more. He would never do that. He never wanted her to feel pressured to change herself, and he would never want her to sacrifice her dreams for his.

The news shouldn't have disturbed him as much as it did, but the message was clear. They could have friendship. Anything else was impossible.

CHAPTER EIGHTEEN

Present Day

NOBI HAD NO concept of time anymore. She only recognized daytime by the sun still in the sky, but it looked to be going down soon. Having finally made it to the house, she dismounted. The stone house was a castle, and it was open and welcoming. It did not look like the place where her best friend might be tortured for information or some item that was not worth his life. The flowers were in bloom and the vibrant fuchsia and yellow blossoms were cheery and bright. The image of it all betrayed the storm thundering in her heart. Her bedraggled clothing and disheveled hair were a far better reflection of the misery and chaos rampant in the air. Thankfully the rain had stopped and she was not dripping wet. She didn't need a crying dress, no matter how much of a relief it might offer her to have something cry for the state she was in.

She knocked on the door. When no one answered, she pushed on the door to go inside. Of course, it was locked. Dash it all!

Bringing the horse out of sight of anyone who might come up to the front of the house, she tied him up and then proceeded to look for another door (or window if need be) to climb into the house. Yes, she was desperate. She was more than willing to climb through a window at this point. In fact, if she had to lose some layers of clothing at this point to squeeze through a crack, she would do it. She was a woman willing to do anything, and that should terrify Chris's captors.

Fortunately, after pushing on a few entrances with no luck, she finally found one at the back of the house. A servant's entrance.

She entered quietly, unsure of what to expect. But the house was eerily silent. No voices. No tapping or clattering. No banging or brushing. No sounds of any kind. If she didn't know better, she would have thought that there was no one in the house at all.

So then…what to do? The ruffians would likely be barging in with Chris in the next short while. Where should she wait? Where she was, the kitchen, seemed as good a place as any. The less time she spent wandering the house, the more time she could spend devising a new plan. All of her former plans required involvement from the staff. With this new turn of events, she was all on her own.

She scanned the kitchen taking note of her surroundings. The bucket of some kind of oil by the door. The cool stove. No one had been in here all afternoon it seemed. Likely some kind of local event was going on. A church event or a fair in the local village. Just her luck. Thankfully there was still a candle burning on the wall to shed some light as evening approached. She watched the light flicker against a glass on the table in the middle of the kitchen. The refracted light sending color in varying directions was at odds with the dismal state of her heart.

Here in the kitchen, there were hazards and opportunities. A kitchen had many sharp tools if she located them first. Nobi took stock of a few knives and a cleaver, placing them beside a seat somewhat out of sight but still able to watch the door. She hoped she wouldn't have to use them. She could hardly imagine doing any damage to a human being with her pistol, least of all with a knife. She shuddered, sending up a prayer again that she wouldn't have to shoot anything. Of late, she really didn't trust her aim.

She settled herself in her chair, taking vigil.

If the captors did come through this door, this location was her best bet at rescuing him. She would have the element of surprise on her side, and if Chris (assuming he was conscious) saw her first, they might be able to work together quickly.

How had life brought her to this point? All she wanted was a nice life in the country with a man she loved. She didn't crave this kind of stimulation. She didn't need to be thrilled or experience new things. She liked safety. Comfort.

But this was Chris...

And she couldn't live without him...

No. She really couldn't. Look at her? She was risking her life for this man. She loved him. And what if she rescued him and they both came out alive? Then what? What was next? Going back to their friendship?

That felt so...hollow. Almost wrong. Their friendship was incredible. It was the single most reliable, heart-warming, inspiring relationship she had outside of her sisters. It was. And now that her sisters were moving on, she needed to as well. That was what the duke dare had been all about. She needed to shoot her shot. And now she might never have the chance to do it.

Because what if one or both of them didn't make it out alive? A tear burned the back of her eye, and her throat throbbed.

That was an unconscionable thought. If he died...she couldn't live.

It was finally her turn at the duke dare, and by God, she would take it.

This was her chance. Life might not give her another one. There might not be more time. She almost wanted to kick herself for wasting so much of it already, but then she realized that if she had changed anything, her sisters might not have all found their true love matches. And their happiness was just as important as hers. So what if she had to sacrifice it for the last several years? Well, now it was her time. Her turn. And she was finally ready to take it.

Nobi withdrew the pistol from behind her pocket and thumbed the rose embellishment. She loved him, and there was a time when she thought he loved her, too. She only hoped she wasn't too late.

She knew it now more than she had ever known before. Her soul, her heart, her body were made for him. Chris was the man she loved and she would give up everything for him. He wanted to travel the world, so she would ask him—beg him—to take her with him. If she could handle a little abduction, surely she could handle a little world traveling. There was no greater uncertainty than risking your life.

Now that her decision was made, there was a fire in Nobi that could not be put out.

After a while, Nobi thought she heard voices heading toward her. She braced her hand on the pistol and sent up another prayer, knowing that in a few minutes she would likely not have the wherewithal to call upon any deities.

Chris crashed through the door first, and she could see his hands were tied and his eyes were as wild as she had ever seen them. He was surveying the room knowing he had only a second to find something, anything, but then his eyes tripped over her. They caught sight of each other, in complete disbelief.

He was alive. She could breathe, for a second. She hadn't realized how much hope she had been clinging to just to be reassured that he was alive. Now that she knew, her hope was rewarded. He was alive. Her heart fluttered. She saw him.

And he saw her, too. His face registering shock, relief, and fear all at the same time. She flashed the pistol at him so that he knew she was armed. He nodded.

Then he tilted his head back and she understood it to mean she should stay hidden, so she pulled back as far as she could into her corner. And just as she did so, a tall lanky man came barreling in behind Chris. Chris tried to dodge him, but his shock combined with the other man's momentum did not pair well for Chris's favor. Immediately, the ruffian threw his arm around Chris's neck and pulled him into his chest.

Nobi gasped at the viciousness of the headlock, but did her utmost to stay invisible.

"What the devil are you doing?" The ruffian grumbled at

Chris. "You thought you could get away, again?"

Chris answered with a grunt, and she could see his eyes flickering about the room. She could tell that he was coming up with a plan, so she followed his eyes.

"It's just us here," Chris's voice came out strained through the chokehold. "Everyone else is at the *fair*." He dropped his voice on the word fair, and Nobi knew he was trying to tell her something. She just had to pay attention to the clues.

"I bet they've all gone to see the *fortuneteller*."

"Shut the hell up. Why are you all of a sudden so chatty?" The captor tightened his grip on Chris.

But Nobi knew he was telling her something. She just had to put the pieces together. The fair. The fortuneteller. That had been one of the best and worst days of her life. She remembered the day in a flash. The fun they had had together. She was sure he was in love with her that day. And even before that. But that day they had been in public. He had bought her the very pistol she was holding right now.

She had won him the globe, which now sat in her bedchambers so she was prepared to follow him and his world traveling.

And then they had visited the blasted fortuneteller. Who had ruined everything. Well, that was dramatic. In actuality, she had just summed up their relationship within thirty seconds. They were opposites, not meant to be together. A next to impossibility.

And Nobi remembered her and Chris's short conversation directly after the visit. They had both chuckled and said it was a good thing they were friends.

Well, she was tired of all the friendship. She wanted more.

And that's when she remembered the fire. The small fire that had occurred from a candle falling to the ground.

She looked up at Chris, trying to hold her position. She raised her brows in question and watched as he guided her with his eyes to the plan he had devised.

Now she knew what he wanted her to do. But she couldn't do it. That shot he wanted her to make? It was far too difficult.

Far too close to his head. Her aim was all off. She couldn't do it. He would have to come up with something else.

"Jax will be here any minute. Then you can show us where the pistols are."

Jax? Another man was coming? Oh God, she needed to make that shot. Could she do it? It didn't matter. She had to do it.

But she had to stand up to do it.

Swiftly, she rose to her feet and took aim.

"Who are you?" the man spluttered.

"I'm the last woman you'd ever want to meet in this abduction. That's my man you're holding."

Chris smirked and nodded slowly. Then he kicked over the bucket of oil and she took her shot.

She took her damn shot. And she kept her eyes open, because whether she lived to tell of it or not, she wanted the last thing she saw to be Chris's face.

Her bullet nicked the candle holder in the perfect spot. It fell into the oil and started a blaze.

Chris bashed his head against the man's nose and jumped over the flames, racing toward her. The next moments were a blur. The ruffian had dropped his gun and was holding his face. He was also doing some frantic-looking jig to get away from the flames, yet he was still caught up in the blaze. While he was sorting through that mess, she sliced through Chris's ropes, and someone (probably Chris) took some powder and threw it on the flames.

"Nice shot by the way. I had no doubt you could make it." He pasted a breezy kiss on her cheek, and then in the next moment, Chris sat atop the man away from the now squelched fire.

"Hand me the rope, Nobi," he instructed. "You're doing great. We're almost out of this mess, darling. Go sit back in that chair and stay out of sight. This won't take long now. Just a little bit more to go."

Then he was tying the ruffian up and pushing him against the wall, out of the way of the doorframe. There was no time for explanations, no time for anything, because then the sounds of a second man were coming toward the door. Ostensibly unaware of all the proceedings that had just taken place, a behemoth of a man surged in, arrogantly looking for Chris who took him out with a single (and surprising) punch to the nose.

More rope. More ties. And then finally, finally, finally, an embrace. No, a kiss. And Chris and Nobi didn't stop kissing until a throat cleared and Cook, while waving a frying pan in the air, said, "Do we need more assistance in here?"

CHAPTER NINETEEN

CHRIS PULLED AWAY from the kiss and looked Nobi in the eyes, and at the precise moment his heart hammered out of his throat with the words, "I have to tell you something."

Nobi expressed the exact same sentiment, "I have to tell you something."

While he stared at her intently he knew this was the moment for him to finally share his heart—

"Ahem." Cook cleared her throat again. "I know there's a lot that needs to be said, and done, between you two, but can we sort out these two buffoons first? I'd rather not have to cook over these two ogres. A lot should be returning shortly in search of dinner, so I'm sure we can round up some footmen to take care of them, but if you want dinner on time—and I'm not sure you do, but if you do—then you'll need to manage the chaos while I manage the kitchen."

The reminder snapped Chris to attention. With Nobi's face still in his hands, he pressed a soft kiss to her cheek. "Soon. Very soon. We'll talk."

Then he went into duke mode as he strode out of the kitchen. The staff would be returning shortly which meant they wouldn't be too far off. Within a minute he caught sight of a footman who he directed to find a few more men. Not soon after that, the stablehands were returning, so he grabbed a few of them to watch the ruffians. Two stood guard while a third went in search of a Bow Street runner.

The events passed quickly, but not quickly enough. Chris ached to finally be with Nobi. It had been too long. He could feel the intense pressure boiling inside of him, keen on bubbling over. The way she had kissed him in the kitchen indicated that she might be of the same mind as he was…but he couldn't help the small skeptic in some dark corner of his mind from leading him astray.

What if that kiss wasn't expressing an undying love so much as it was expressing relief, gratitude, and joy that he was safe? God only knows how he would feel if the roles had been reversed. If Nobi's life was in danger…he exhaled a ragged sigh…he wouldn't know what to do with himself.

They had kissed countless times in the past. Perhaps they had defaulted to that mode of being? Perhaps she was comforting him in the only way she knew how? Perhaps all the anxiety of the abduction was squelched, just like that fire was, with a kiss?

No. He couldn't think that way. He had to stay optimistic. Even if it was a kiss of friendship. That wasn't the kiss of death. He could still tell her how he felt, ask her to marry him—nay, convince her to marry him—and then spend the rest of his life wooing her until she fell head over feet for him.

He didn't need anything else in the world except to love her.

And that's what he reminded himself of as he stormed back into the house. He was still a man on a mission. His freedom was only the first half. Seeing her, loving her, that was the rest of the mission.

When he reached the house the same way he left, he expected to see Nobi in the kitchen. Although, if he thought about it, it didn't really make sense that she would have just waited there, pistol in hand, for him.

So when she wasn't standing there, pistol—or otherwise—in hand for him, he demanded, "Where is she?"

Cook gave him a wry look, "What did you expect? That she would sit in the corner awaiting your return?"

No. Obviously he didn't expect that. She was a woman of action, if anything…he felt like an idiot thinking it…she would have been standing. But not to go down that circular route again, he asked again. "Well, where is she?"

"The poor woman was shaken up. She's in the pink bedchamber taking a bath, resting."

Chris took a few steps to storm after her.

"You're going to see her now?" Cook, who was really only getting away with this attitude because she had been around when he was in leading strings begging for cookies, needled him.

"I don't care if the woman is naked. I'm going to her now." And then just to be sure Cook knew his intentions were honorable—because he couldn't disappoint the one who had gone out of her way to make his favorite oatmeal cookies growing up, he added, "I'm going to make her my wife."

Cook clucked her tongue, "I'm not stopping you. I was just asking." Then she gave him a wink. "What are you waiting for? Go get her."

Chris shot like a bullet up the stairs and burst into her room. And sure enough, though she gasped loudly when she saw him, she was sitting in a large copper bath pouring water over her shoulders. Her bare shoulders. Shoulders that he had seen before. Kissed before. Marked before. Loved before. But it was all nothing compared to how he felt now.

Now he needed to make those shoulders his wife. Uh. That woman with those shoulders, and that great big heart.

Why had he waited so long? A tear burned the corner of his eye. He needed her to be his.

He dropped to his knees beside her.

"Chris? What are you doing here?"

"We need to talk."

"It couldn't wait." She said it as a statement, not a question. And that observation gave him hope.

Before he could get out a single word, she blurted out, "Take me with you."

And though he was sure he knew what she meant, he asked anyway, "Where?"

"Everywhere you plan to go."

His heart soared above, far higher than any clouds he had witnessed. "When?"

"Whenever you want. I'm ready."

He cupped her cheek, his fingertips playing with the damp hair at the nape of her neck. "Nobi, I don't need to spend my whole life traveling. I no longer need to go anywhere but with you. I don't need to see everything. I just want to see you every day."

She sighed his name.

"I love you, Nobi. I always have and I always will."

"Always?" she asked breathlessly, as though in disbelief.

"Since the moment we faked a tryst to save me from that husband-hunter."

"You did?"

He nodded. And when her warm wet thumbs rubbed at his cheeks, he realized that the wetness wasn't just from her fingers. A few tears were streaking down his cheeks.

"It's always been you, Nobi. I-I I haven't been with anyone since I've been with you."

Her gasp caught him off guard. He never would have thought that she would expect him to be faithful to her and their friendship, but her gasp of delight told him that she loved him all the more for his loyalty.

But they had always known that. Always known that of each other. They were loyal. Protective. They would do nothing to hurt the other person.

"You really love me?" Her eyes shone with tears now too, and it was his turn to kiss them away.

"I love you more than I've ever loved anything, Nobi. You are my greatest adventure."

"I love you. You are my rock," she whispered and pulled his lips to hers.

"You're my light. There's never been anyone else that has caught my soul the way you have."

"Nor me," she kissed his cheek. When she pulled back, she had a cheeky grin on her face. One of her hands drifted from his face to his fingers, and she tucked her pinky inside of his until she had him wrapped. "But what about those thousand needles?"

His smile couldn't have grown any wider. "We will always have our friendship. There's no need for any needle-swallowing. You are my best friend. You will always be. But now you will be my wife."

At those words, she held in a sob.

Thankfully the tub was large. Chris stood up and crawled in, one knee down in the tub. Water splashed over the edges. He didn't care. If the recent sequence of events had taught him anything, it was to live. Live now. There was no better time than now. It was the present. And he wanted to open it and appreciate it for all it was worth.

"Nobi, you are my greatest joy. Every memory we have together, I cherish because you are my treasure. I will devote my life to protecting you, being loyal to you, exploring the adventure that is you. Loving you with my body, mind, heart, and soul. You are my everything. My friend, my lover. Will you do me the greatest honor and become my wife?"

"Yes!" she shouted, and water splashed around them as she took to her knees and threw her arms around his neck.

Her lips were finding his and the kisses were sloppy. Ravenous. Full of hunger and passion. And he knew that his life would never be the same.

"I wasn't ready before," she murmured in between kisses.

"It doesn't matter, we're ready now. We're both here now." He reassured her with his words and with kisses trailing down her neck. She smelled of his fresh soap and he wanted to feast on her.

"I wasn't ready before, but now I am. I had to almost lose you"—her voice choked up—"before I could grasp hold of you. I will never let you go, Chris."

"You couldn't let me go if you tried, my treasure." He took her nipple into his mouth and lightly sucked on her.

"Uh…Chris. I love you. I would give up everything for you."

"You don't have to." Saying the words gave him a small break as well as a good excuse to transfer his attention to her other breast.

"That may be, but I want you to know that I would. My life needs you in it to feel full. It's hollow without you."

She was peeling back his now heavy layers of clothing, but the fabric was sticking to him, making it a nearly impossible task for one person to accomplish.

"Together," he said with two meanings as he started to help shuck his layers to the floor, "we can do anything. Together."

When his top layers were removed, he leaned in for a kiss, but Nobi's hands on his chest stopped him.

"Wait," she panted and gestured toward his breeches. "Take those off. Now."

He loved how demanding she was when she was aroused. He stood up, letting the water sluice down his body. With a teasing look, he slowly slid his breeches down. Sopping wet, he let them fall to the floor.

Her hands were around his thighs, and she licked his cock. "I want to taste you, Chris."

His hands flew to the sides of the tub as he arched his hips toward her. She placed kisses along his length and ran her tongue on the underside of his cock. Then she took his head in her mouth and sucked on him. Slowly at first. Gentle. Then she hallowed out her cheeks and slid his tip to the back of her throat.

A harsh moan rattled through the air. "Nobi, I love this. I love you. I want to come inside of you."

She hummed her consent.

"Inside of you to fill you up."

Understanding dawned and she sucked off of him with a pop.

His lips scrambled to find hers and he could taste himself on her lips. His cock was as solid as a gun ready to shoot.

He grabbed her legs and pulled them over his hips. The water was sloshing everywhere as he thrust inside of her.

Her head lolled back and she sobbed her pleasure, encouraging him to take her hard again.

"I need you, Nobi. We'll never be apart again. You're mine. All mine."

He could feel her clenching around him as she moaned. Her legs trembled around his waist and he knew she was close.

"Come for me, my love. My life. My treasure."

With a scream of his name, he felt her pulsate around him, squeezing him, wringing out his pleasure. A flash of white shot through him like a bullet, tearing him up, showing him exactly what he was made of. Flesh and fire.

$$- \text{\textcircled{} } -$$

CHAPTER TWENTY

S IX DAYS LATER, Chris stood in the parlor with his three best friends (besides Nobi) in the whole world. It had been far too long since he'd seen them, but there was no better way to usher in his new life with Nobi than with Wes, James, and Sam.

Wes smacked him on the back, "Trust you to get yourself abducted."

Not one to throw a friend under the carriage, Chris was going to keep his mouth shut, but Sam said it anyway. "It shouldn't have been you. It should have been me." He was shaking his head.

"Don't worry about it. It all happened for many reasons, one of which was so I could find out the truth about your father's death. He didn't kill that man. Big Tall Tom took them both out. Rumor has it he lost his mind. He's gone now too."

"I hate that you went through that, but I'm relieved to know the truth about my father."

"We're all happy to know the truth about your father. He was a good man, despite his flaws." Chris gave Sam an embrace and then stepped back. "Also, apparently I needed the abduction as an excuse to figure out my life and what I wanted with Nobi."

"You sure you needed that drastic of an incident, Chris? You couldn't have required a simple slug to the face or something less dramatic?" James put his two fists up and faked a pugilistic pose.

Sam grabbed him by the jaw, "And wreck this beautiful face? I don't think so. Maybe it did all happen for a reason."

"It did. And I couldn't be happier."

"Well, we can see that," Wes said. "Now where are those pistols?"

"Safe." Chris gestured to the air, indicating they were still locked away. "You can take them when you leave."

"No. I won't be taking those. They belong to Sam."

"What? No, they're yours now."

"I don't think so. You're the one that won the bet from the beginning of the summer."

"Did I? Or did you?" Wes volleyed back.

Sam scratched his head, legitimately befuddled.

"Never mind. The pistols are yours. I don't know why you wagered them in the first place. We should have stuck to pounds, not pistols."

"I thought it would bring me better luck to get rid of them, especially at the time thinking my cousin had ramped up his efforts to take me out," Sam justified.

"Well, did it bring you better luck?" James asked with a smirk on his face.

"Actually, in the most roundabout way it did. Look at us. We're all marrying for love. And we didn't even all believe in it," he slugged James in the arm.

"Oomph. True," he said, rubbing his arm, "but I'm a believer now. I'm just as lovesick as the rest of you sorry three."

A round of laughter rippled through the room.

"But there's one thing I have to get off my chest," Chris said.

"What's that?" James asked, taking a sip of his whiskey.

"You guys were wrong six years ago."

"I don't think so." Wes puffed out his chest.

"You don't even know what I'm referring to."

Wes rubbed his jaw, "But I still don't think we were all wrong."

Chris scoffed. "You warned me not to pursue things with Zenobia."

"Did we?" James tapped his chin.

"Yes, you did."

Perhaps sensing Chris's growing agitation, Sam wrapped his arm around his shoulder. "Did we or didn't we? Maybe we did." Sam patted Chris's stomach like a man would rub a dog's belly to placate him. "We were just looking out for one of our dearest friends. And just think, if we didn't warn you, you might have gone after her too early, and then where would the rest of us sorry lot be?"

Chris regained his internal equanimity. Maybe the belly rub had helped. "True...I guess I was the sacrificial lamb of the group—and," he lifted his hand to stop any rebuttals, "if anyone had to be the one put to slaughter, it may as well have been me. The rest of you would have been bleating far too loudly for us to go through with it anyway."

"Har. Har." Sam joked. "Now, onto more important matters." He pulled a wad of bills from his pockets.

"What the devil is that for? Do we have some outstanding bet I don't know about?" Wes whistled at the bills adding up.

"Not yet," Sam rejoined. "But I plan to place our biggest wager yet."

James's eyes lit up like a twenty-four candle chandelier. "What are we betting on now?"

"What else is there to bet on?" He eyed the other three, waiting for one of them to supply the answer, but Chris was at a loss. Apparently, so were the other three, so Sam announced it for himself. "Babies! Who's going to be the first father among us?"

Laughter cracked, and backs were slapped. Bets were made, and drinks were poured. Then James placed a tumbler in Chris's hand, and Chris raised it into the air. "Here's to four lucky Betting Buddies who finally claimed love."

THE DIAMOND TWINKLED in the sunlight almost as brightly as Nobi's smile. She was engaged. Chris was going to be her husband. And soon! It had only taken six years and an abduction to make them see the truth. Well, perhaps not so much *see* the truth as *act upon* it. They were lovers in the deepest sense of the word, and in a few short hours they were going to be united for all the world to see.

Immediately after Chris had asked her to marry him, she had sent word to her sisters. All right, not immediately after he asked. There had been a few more rounds of love-making, and more than a few bursts of pleasure. Then, after those awe-inspiring rounds, she had written her missives and sent them off.

All of her sisters had replied that they would travel to Chris's house for the wedding. The double wedding! Joan and James would be getting married as well. Even their father would be in attendance.

They had all arrived yesterday to what already felt like her home.

KNOCK. KNOCK.

"Come in!" Nobi called out as three giggling women skipped into the room. They were acting like giddy schoolgirls about to be asked to dance by a boy with the size of the grins on their faces.

"It's our wedding day," Joan announced jubilantly.

Nobi threw her arms around Joan. "Yes. And I'm so excited to share this day with you. I missed you so much."

Mimi jumped in on the hug. "What about me? Did you miss me too?"

Boudicca tsked the youngest but also joined in on the hug. "We all missed each other, and we're all excited to be here together again." She wiped a tear from her eye.

Nobi craned her neck for a better view. "Bodi, are you crying?"

"Quite possibly. Marriage might have softened me a touch," she sniffled. "I'm just so happy for you." Another sniff. "For all of us."

"Marriage doesn't soften you, it makes you braver," Mimi said, patting the eldest's shoulder, still in the group's embrace. "Every day you have to choose to trust. Choose to open your heart. Choose to love."

"You've become wiser in your married state, Mimi," Bodi said encouragingly.

"I've always been this wise, you just didn't all always recognize it," she smirked.

"We must be the luckiest four sisters in the world," Joan added. "To think we are all four marrying for love, and to each a handsome duke."

With an over-satisfied grin, Mimi said wryly, "I think we need to thank Zenobia for her cowardice with Chris."

"Cowardice? I'm insulted."

"Cowardice? Timidity? Procrastination? What would you call it?"

"I call it…playing the long game."

The sisters laughed.

"Well, whatever you call it, I'm glad you did it." Mimi tightened her hold on them and then let go to sit on Nobi's bed. "I am sorry you had to go through this terrible ordeal with Chris being abducted though. Of all the sisters to have to go through it…"

The other three clamored onto the bed and sat cross-legged, just as they had always done. "I know what you mean, Mimi. I can't believe it happened to me."

Joan reached out and pressed a tender hand on her forearm. "How was it? Are you all right?"

Nobi squeezed her eyes shut and exhaled. "It was terrifying. I've never experienced so much fear." With a deep inhalation, she continued. "But I had no choice. Or I guess, I felt as though I had no choice. Chris needed me." Her voice dropped to a whisper, "And I needed him."

"That must have taken everything you had inside of you to go after him," Bodi said with pride.

"That and then some. I never knew what I had inside of me. I never knew what I was capable of. A-a-and…just before this all happened, I had lost my ability to shoot at a target."

"What do you mean?" Mimi asked in shock. "You've never not been able to hit a bullseye."

"I know. I think with everything that was going on and feeling so much loss around me, my mind was unfocused. Cloudy. I couldn't see what I wanted. The bullseye. I was going out that morning to practice my shot when I overheard the plan to kidnap someone. I didn't know it was going to be Chris. But when I rode out after him for his help and saw them take him, my heart leapt into my throat. I had so few options. None it felt. So I followed them."

"You're so brave, Nobi," Joan said.

"I had to be. I couldn't let him…die." Her throat choked up as she willed away the desolate thought, thankful it wasn't a reality anymore. "Anyway, like Mimi was saying about choices…I had to choose. I had to trust myself and go after him."

"And then when you finally caught up with him?"

"It felt like an eternity had passed. And I saw my life play out both ways: without him and with him. I knew I couldn't live without him anymore, so I planned to tell him how I felt."

"But how did he get free?" Bodi asked.

"I shot a candle."

"A candle?"

"Yes, thankfully Chris had a plan and gave me some hints. And then I took my shot and I hit the target I wanted to. It was like I could see what I needed to have and nothing was going to keep me from getting it."

"I love this new side of you, Nobi," Joan said encouragingly. "You're stronger than you ever thought you were. You've always been quieter, a little bit like me, but that doesn't make us weak. We're resolute. Determined. And when we know what we want, we can go after it. Whatever it is."

"Yes." Nobi's heart was full as she smiled at her sisters. "And now we have to put the final claim on that, don't we, Joan? Shall we get ready for our wedding?"

The joy that filled the room was unspeakable. It resounded in laughter and tears. Embraces and memories.

As the sisters dressed, they cooed over how gorgeous the dresses looked, Nobi in a blue dress and Joan in green, the other sisters wore a pale pink. For flowers, they chose wild flowers.

When Bodi put their mother's bracelet on Nobi's wrist, and their mother's earrings on Joan, all four were in tears. "Mother would be so proud of us. She would be here with a hug and a kind word for both of you."

Sniffles filled the room.

"And she wouldn't have told us anything about what to expect in the bedroom," Mimi teased, which elicited laughter from all of them.

Bodi spoke once the laughter faded, "This is the one of the most special days of your lives, you two. You get to claim the men you love. And they will claim you. From this day forward, you will protect each other, love each other, challenge each other, and lean on each other. We four will always be sisters, but our relationships will change. They'll deepen, even though we're further away from each other. We'll learn to grow together in a whole new way. Of course we can complain to each other about our husband's when they eat too loudly—it will happen—but we will also celebrate each milestone in our lives together. Our new homes, our children, birthdays, anniversaries, and more."

Bodi grabbed some filled flutes of champagne that had been brought in by a servant. "This is to our new beginning."

"To love," Nobi said.

"To laughter," Joan said.

"To happily ever after," Mimi said.

EPILOGUE I

THE DOUBLE WEDDING had been better than anything Chris could have imagined. He thought back to the day with pure pleasure. Many kinds of pleasure, but foremost in his mind was how much of a treasure he had found in Zenobia.

After securing a special license, she had walked down the makeshift aisle of his garden toward him wearing a blue that made her eyes shimmer. Her smile lit up his heart, and it floated above the clouds up into the space filled with stars and dreams.

When he held her hands in his to repeat his vows, he knew again without doubt that she was the one for him. *For better or worse, richer or poorer, sickness or health, to love and to cherish, till death us do part, according to God's holy ordinance, I vow to be faithful…*There was no question in his mind that they would take care of each other. They always had, and they always would.

Sliding the ring on her finger had made him the happiest man in the world, or perhaps the galaxy. He had always thought of her as his, but now she was. And the whole world would know it. There were no more questions or doubts in his mind. No more fears about losing her or damaging their friendship. Their friendship was intact, stronger than ever, and they were building upon it as the foundation for their marriage.

It had taken a long time for them to get to this place, but he wouldn't change a thing because it meant that his friends had found love and happiness as well.

James and Joan couldn't have been happier with the arrangement, and their father had made a touching toast that included their mother. Chris would never forget the words he said, "Love is a rare gift. If you find it, treasure it. But don't hide it, share it. The more you love, the more capable you are to love even more."

He wasn't a man of many words, somewhat like Chris himself, and when he spoke, his daughter's listened with their hearts.

And those words registered deeply with him because Zenobia was his treasure. He had always thought of her as such.

After the wedding, the two newlyweds had departed (separately) for their honeymoons. And surprisingly, Zenobia had insisted they visit the continent.

Apparently she wanted to travel with him. She had said his dreams were important to her, so here they stood, on a ferry to Calais, France and then off to Paris. Perhaps more. Since this trip wasn't so much for sightseeing, they were planning it as they went.

With the wind in her hair, he looked over at Zenobia. His wife. His beautiful wife with a sparkle in her eye. She was up to something.

"What are you thinking about?" he prompted her.

"Just a little something from our past." Given how many memories that had swamped him lately, he couldn't imagine that she would bring up something he hadn't thought of in vivid detail.

"What's that?"

"I've always been curious about it. I'm hoping you can tell me now. What did you wish for that night when we saw the shooting star?" Zenobia asked him with a cheeky, hopeful, little grin.

Given what they had gone through, he didn't think it necessary to keep his wish to himself anymore, so he decided to share it with her. "I wished that you would always be brave and take the shots you wanted to take in life."

Zenobia's eyes welled with tears, and she interlaced her fingers with his. He pulled her into his chest and kissed her hair. "What did you wish for, my treasure?"

Sotto voce, she said, "I wished for you to never give up on your dreams."

And he squeezed her tighter.

"Is that why we're here?"

"Partly," she said in a rough whisper, "and partly to show you how much I love you."

"I know how much you love me. You risked your life for me. You shot a man for me."

She slapped his arm. "I didn't shoot a man. I shot above him. Like you told me too."

He teasingly rubbed his jaw, "I suppose I did do that. Good thing we paid that visit to the fortuneteller then, otherwise I might not have thought of that plan so quickly on my feet."

"Hmmm…about that fortuneteller, she was so wrong about us."

"Yes, I gave her and her words some thought through this whole ordeal. And I keep coming back to her saying that it was next to impossible, yet it was a choice."

"It's a good thing we chose each other then, and didn't heed her words." Nobi slipped her hands around Chris's waist and pressed a kiss against his neck. No one was around, and even if they were, he didn't think she would have noticed.

"Or perhaps next to impossible is the perfect place to be."

"Yes, there's that…"

"Or?"

"Well, there's another place I wouldn't mind being." She hinted with her eyebrows and he scooped her up carrying them to the little room he had secured. Foresight told him they might need some privacy, even on the short jaunt across the water.

Once he had her in the room, he kicked the door shut.

"Tell me more about that place you want to be, Nobi."

"I think I could be…here," she leaned against the door he had just slammed shut, and he growled in response. "Or…I could be here…" she sat down on one of the chairs and casually spread her legs. When he moaned, she stood up quickly and made her way to the small cot. "But I really think I'd like to be here right now." Button by button, she slowly started to undo the side of her dress. Chris was there in a flash.

"I need to be here, too." His fingers peeled back the layers of her dress, and then he slipped one finger between the valley of her breasts. "And I need to be here." She mewled in response. "And I need to be here," he said, dragging his finger down to her core.

"I vowed to obey you," she murmured.

"And I vowed to cherish you, let me show you how much I can cherish you." He took her mouth in his and on her gasp, he swirled his tongue into her mouth. She sucked on him and nibbled on his bottom lip, grasping at his head, holding him close.

Her passion fueled the already lit flame inside of him and his cocked swelled, knowing where this kiss was headed.

"You're my love," she whispered into his ear.

"You're my dream," he whispered back.

Gently, he laid her down on the bed. Layer by layer, he peeled off his clothes until his chest puffed out instinctively with pride that she was his. And then his cock bobbed up to show her how beyond control his feelings were for her.

"You're even more beautiful to me today than the day I met you. I'll never stop loving you."

In reply, she reached up and pulled him back down for a kiss.

His cock nestled between her legs, he could feel her entire body tremble at his touch. Her hands flew to his backside, demanding, and her legs opened wide, making room for him.

Then her heels locked around his lower back and she lifted her hips to his, searching for his manhood.

"A lady was never meant to be so wanton as I am with you." She shuddered when his tip notched at her entrance.

"You're my lady, and you can be however you want." He

pressed a kiss to her neck.

"Mark me as yours, Chris," she begged him.

And his teeth sunk into her neck, sucking hard until he knew he had fulfilled her request.

"Take me to the place only you can," she pleaded, pushing up and taking him into her.

He groaned at the feel of her all around him. "You're so wet, so tight, so perfect for me."

"You're perfect for me."

He thrust into her, and each time she rose to meet him, her breaths grew shorter and faster.

"Chris, I-I-I'm coming. Ooooh," she squealed her pleasure and that sound wrapped tightly around his cock at the same time she clenched his quim around him. Together they came, reaching new heights of euphoria. Never had he felt so complete, so happy, so fully himself and loved. This was an adventure he wanted to take over and over again.

He was hers, and she was his forever.

And it was perfect.

And they were perfect for each other the rest of their days, the Duke and his lady.

EPILOGUE II

"THE PICNIC IS ready, Nobi," Chris said, giving her a kiss on the cheek and a gentle rub on her belly. He squeezed her close. "I have a little treat for you, my treasure." He pulled a petit four from the palm of his hand and let her take a bite.

"Delicious," she moaned.

"Shall we go see your family or sneak up to our room?"

"Or shall we take to the fields again?" she winked at him.

It was a beautiful summer afternoon, the wind was a soft breeze through the trees while the sun shone enough to warm the skin but not scorch it. It was a perfect day.

She gave into his kiss for a lingering minute and then playfully swatted his hands away. "As much as I'd like for you to take me today—again—I think we should visit with family. Especially since they all made the effort to be here."

He chuckled and laced his fingers into hers. "Let's go."

Together they traversed down into the garden where everyone was waiting.

The happy chatter reached their ears. Talk of memories filtered the air.

"How was the one-month-turned-several-months trip around the continent?" James jokingly asked the hosts.

"It was," Nobi gazed up at Chris and took a breath, "exceptional."

"This one here would have kept traveling, but I had to remind her that we had family back home that we should probably see." Chris nudged her in the ribs.

"Yes, I probably could have stayed a little bit longer, at least for that first trip, but I'm more than happy to be home. Now I know that we can travel whenever we want to."

"Yes," Chris placed a kiss on her cheek, "and we will. We might even take a trip with your father who's still gallivanting about."

"He's always somewhere," she laughed. "And I think he wouldn't mind the company once in a while."

"But now that we're home, I'm happy to be here."

"Well, we're glad you invited us for the day," Wes said. "We owe you two so much."

"Yes, you two and the duke dare," James whistled, "we all owe everything to the duke dare."

"The duke dare?" Chris raised his eyebrows. "What's the duke dare?"

Wes, Sam, and James all three exchanged a curious glance and Nobi felt a nervous flutter in her stomach.

"You know," Mimi waved her hand in the air as if that explained everything, "the duke dare."

"No, I don't know the duke dare."

"Ooh," Mimi threw a hand over her eyes.

Joan sucked in a breath and Bodi closed her eyes in a long, slow blink.

"Oh…um…yes, the duke dare, well, you know, nothing really to say about that." Nobi picked up a piece of bread and added some cheese to it before she popped it into her mouth—or was that a biscuit? It didn't matter. At least her mouth was busy, as she made the world's worst attempt at explaining something she didn't want to unpack. "Mhmmfmmp…wmmmfpw."

"Nobi, I can wait until you've finished your biscuit and cheese combination." He stood with his hands on his hips. She hadn't seen him look that severe in a while. Sometimes in the bedroom he adopted an authoritative role. Her cheeks flushed. Now was clearly not the time for those thoughts.

Or was it?

She swallowed the lump of food she had chewed and reached for Chris. Whispering in his ear, she said, "I think I'd like to take you up on that offer now to roll around in the grass."

Loudly, Chris answered, "Oh no, you don't. There's something you're all not telling me." He pointed his finger around the group as they all simultaneously sipped their drinks. "What is this duke dare business all about?"

Aside, Mimi whispered to Nobi, "You never told him?"

"I thought I did…but I guess I didn't. And then I just never thought about it again."

"Oh my," Joan said, shaking her head.

"Well, you see…" Nobi nibbled on her bottom lip. "You know I love you dear."

"Yes, yes. Get on with it." He made a rolling gesture with his hand. After that signal, Nobi wasn't sure if she preferred his hands on his hips or not.

"Well…all right…you know I love you. I always have." She rushed to continue so that he wouldn't interrupt. "And I just, well, I didn't want to lose you as a friend, but I was too…"

"Shy?"

"Fearful?"

"Cowardly?"

All her sisters supplied those answers. And though it probably didn't matter, the order of the corresponding sisters was: Joan, Bodi, and then Mimi.

"Yes, that." She glared at them. "Thank you, for *that*." She cleared her throat. "Well, apparently I needed a little bit of a push, some motivation so to speak, so that I would finally make a move with you."

"We all dared each other to snag a duke," Mimi said, triumphantly. "And then we all did. With"—she pointed her finger in the air—"true love." Then she bowed. "Thank you very much."

"So I'm a dare then, am I?" Chris narrowed his eyes at her.

"Well, yes, but no. Oh, what a mess." Chris stalked toward her and she slowly backed up with each step he took.

"Nobi," his voice was low and rumbling as he took another step.

"It was never a dare to go after you. That was all my heart telling me what to do. I love you—"

"I know."

"And well, I would have told you—wait, what?"

"I know you love me." His eyes softened and his hands slipped around her waist. "And I knew about the duke dare."

Her eyes flew wide. "You did?"

When he laughed, she cupped his jaw. "The men told me all about it."

"They did?"

"And it wasn't a big deal at all. That's why I never brought it up."

"What a joke to play on a pregnant lady." She swatted his shoulder.

"Yipes!" he said, feigning injury.

"Pregnant?" Mimi shrieked and jumped up running to her sister. "Ah, you're pregnant."

Nobi's face beamed. "We were going to tell you all this afternoon."

All of her sisters surrounded her with an embrace. The men congratulated Chris.

"Nobi, I'm so excited for you. How far along are you?" Bodi asked, her cheeks red.

"I think I'm about twelve weeks, but I'm not sure."

Wes stepped up behind Bodi and wrapped his arms around her. His nose nuzzled into her neck, and he placed a kiss on her throat and then whispered something in her ear.

"We weren't going to say anything for a few more weeks…but…we're about nine weeks along," Bodi announced.

"What?" Nobi squealed in disbelief. "You're pregnant, too?" A tear threatened to spill over her eyes. She wasn't losing her sisters, they were growing their families. Together.

Mimi and Sam were in a back to chest embrace as well, when he kissed her temple.

"Don't forget about us!" Mimi shouted amidst the ongoing congratulations. "We're about ten weeks along."

"Oh all right," Joan mumbled after a nudge from James.

"She's got a bun in the oven, too!" James shouted.

Joan blushed. "Yes, we're going to have a baby. We're about ten weeks along."

"Oh my heavens!" Nobi cried. "This is the absolute best news I have ever heard. We're all going to be mothers together."

The sisters were all in tears, no one knew whose handkerchief belonged to whom anymore. Joy filled their hearts and love abounded.

"I see how it is, last to wed but first to father. Well, done, Duke."

Nobi let the moment wash over her. She never would have believed she could be so happy. There was a time when she thought that the best life she could have was with Chris as her friend. Now he was her husband and he was going to be a father. The father of her child. Life was full of passion, loyalty, and intimacy. They were committed to each other forever. She couldn't imagine any greater joy. No greater purpose than to love and love some more. Love greatly, love deeply, love recklessly, above all.

This was what life was about. Four sisters who dared each other to be brave enough and to dream big enough. To settle for nothing less than love and their best possible lives. And of course, she couldn't not mention those four betting buddies, who never saw it coming.

About the Author

Eliana Piers, award-winning and international best-selling author, has been writing and singing stories since she was five years old. After feeling inspired by authors like Julia Quinn, Tessa Dare, and Minerva Spencer, Eliana decided to test her quill on the page.

Writing about love and how two people come to connect and share parts of their souls with each other is now an obsession.

It's not worth it if you don't laugh, learn, or love while you're in it.

Eliana lives in Canada where she drinks an iced cap every day.

www.ingramcontent.com/pod-product-compliance
Lightning Source LLC
Chambersburg PA
CBHW072139300726
48975CB00003B/1127